THE PENTAGON SPY

THE HARDY BOYS™ MYSTERY STORIES

THE PENTAGON SPY

Franklin W. Dixon

**Illustrated by
Leslie Morrill**

WANDERER BOOKS
Published by Simon & Schuster, New York

Manufactured in the United States of America
1   2   3   4   5   6   7   8   9   10

Wanderer and colophon are trademarks
of Simon & Schuster

Library of Congress Cataloging in Publication Data

Dixon, Franklin W
The pentagon spy.

(His Hardy boys mystery stories; 61)
SUMMARY: Valuable antique weathervanes are being
stolen in the Pennsylvania Dutch country. A Navy employee
removes a top secret document from the Pentagon. The Hardy
brothers try to solve these two seemingly unrelated mysteries.
     [1.   Mystery and detective stories]   I.   Morrill,
Leslie H.   II.   Title.
PZ7.D644Pe   [Fic]   79-24463

ISBN   0-671-95562-4
ISBN   0-671-95570-5 pbk.

Also available in Wanderer Reinforced Edition

Contents

1

Spies, Submarines, and Sailboats

"This case is a tough one, boys," said Fenton Hardy, the famous private detective, after he had settled himself comfortably behind the desk in his study. "It concerns our government and possibly a foreign power. Espionage in Washington, that's what it looks like at this point."

His sons, Frank and Joe, who were seated in two leather chairs facing their father, perked up.

"Can you tell us more about it, Dad, or is it classified?" asked dark-haired Frank, who was a senior in high school.

"If so, we won't ask any questions," added Joe, who was blond and a year younger. But he sounded disappointed.

1

Mr. Hardy smiled. "I've cleared you with the Defense Department," he said, "because you may be in on this before it's over. I may need your help."

"Great!" Joe said excitedly. "What's your case about?"

"A spy in the Pentagon," Mr. Hardy replied.

The boys looked at one another in amazement.

"How could a spy get through all that clearance?" Frank asked. "They check everybody in the Pentagon, from the brass on down."

Mr. Hardy nodded. "That's what the Defense Department wants me to investigate. How did a spy manage to operate under their noses?"

"Any suspects?" Joe inquired. Like Frank, he was always eager for a mystery.

Mr. Hardy nodded. "A civilian employee of the navy named Clifford Hunter has disappeared. So has a top-secret navy document. It appears that Hunter sneaked the document out of the files and smuggled it out of the Pentagon."

Frank whistled. "He must be a cool customer! Any clues, Dad?"

"Yes. The FBI traced Hunter to Chesapeake Bay. We know he shoved off into the bay aboard his sailboat. Since then—nothing. The navy's asked me to enter the case because I've done investigations for them in the past."

"Tell us about this guy Hunter," Frank urged.

Fenton Hardy explained that the suspect was a physicist assigned to computer programming for underwater guidance systems. "This is a real break-through by navy scientists. It gives our command-ers of nuclear submarines pinpoint navigational accuracy on around-the-globe voyages half a mile below the surface of the ocean."

"Wow!" Joe exclaimed. "A sub could leave Bay-port and hit Easter Island right on the nose without taking a single breath! I'll bet it would make those stone heads talk to one another!" He was referring to the South Pacific island whose ancient popula-tion was known for carving remarkable stone monuments.

Fenton Hardy smiled at his son's enthusiasm. "The scientific details are even more dramatic than that, Joe. But you boys know enough now to realize what the navy's up against. The document Hunter took must be recovered before it reaches a foreign government."

"Maybe a gang of foreign agents is mixed up in the case!" Joe said. He was more impetuous than Frank, who did not jump to conclusions so quickly. They had solved many cases together and had helped their father with some of his investigations.

Fenton Hardy was a former member of the New York Police Department, who now worked out of Bayport as a private investigator. He had achieved national fame and put many notorious public enemies behind bars.

Joe's exclamation made his father frown. "It's possible that foreign agents are involved," he said. "That's why I may need you and Frank to help me. If Hunter's planning to turn the sub document over to them, we must stop him before he succeeds. Here's an identification card for each of you. Carry it with you wherever you go." He handed the boys two plastic-encased cards with their pictures on them.

Just then Mrs. Hardy entered the room. She was an attractive, pleasant woman who often worried about the cases her husband and sons investigated.

"Fenton," she announced, "your suitcase is ready. I've packed everything you'll need for a week."

"Thank you, my dear," the detective replied. Rising to his feet, he handed Joe a piece of paper. "Here's the telephone number at the Pentagon where you can reach me. Check with me tomorrow and I'll let you know how the Hunter case is progressing."

He started to leave, then remembered something and turned back to his sons. "By the way," he said, "I have an appointment here this morning with a man named John Hammerley. Make my apologies, will you?"

Then he went out of the room. Shortly afterward, the sound of his car rolling down the driveway into Elm Street indicated that he was on his way to the airport to catch a plane to Washington.

Frank and Joe discussed the mystery of the spy in the Pentagon, who had disappeared with the classified navy document.

"I wonder where he went," Frank said thoughtfully. "He couldn't really go too far in a sailboat."

"People have sailed all the way to Europe," Joe reminded him.

"While carrying a classified stolen document?" Frank shook his head. "Hardly. But he could have met a foreign agent out on the bay."

"We won't know until we get an SOS from Dad," Joe said. "And then we'll have to be ready to move in."

"I hope that won't be necessary," Mrs. Hardy said in a worried tone.

"It's all right, Mom," Frank reassured her. "Dad's got the navy behind him. And I'd sure hate to buck the U.S. Navy."

Mr. Hardy's sister, who lived with the family, stuck her head through the open door. "Spies, submarines, sailboats!" she exclaimed. "What's next?"

The boys grinned. They knew their aunt was very fond of them even though she had a tart tongue and often criticized her nephews.

"How about a piece of chocolate pie, Aunt Gertrude?" Joe suggested.

"Humph! It's certainly better for you than getting involved with spies!" Miss Hardy declared. Then she smiled and led the way to the kitchen, where she served her nephews a sample of her excellent culinary skills.

"You two mind the store now," Aunt Gertrude commanded. "Your mother and I have some shopping to do."

"Don't worry, we will," Joe said as he took a soda out of the refrigerator.

Fifteen minutes later the doorbell rang. Frank went to answer it. A dignified man in a brown suit stood outside. He was wearing a deerstalker hat with a high crown and a peak in front.

"He must have borrowed that hat from Sherlock Holmes," Frank thought while he greeted the stranger with a smile.

The man removed his hat. "Is this the Hardy residence?" he inquired.

"It is, sir," Frank replied.

The visitor handed him a card bearing the name John Hammerley, Lancaster, Pennsylvania.

"Young man, may I come in?" he asked in a troubled tone of voice.

"Of course, Mr. Hammerley. We've been expecting you." Frank stepped aside and ushered their visitor into the living room. There he introduced himself and Joe, and the three sat down.

"I'm a Pennsylvania farmer with an office in the city of Lancaster where I deal in grain," Hammerley announced. "I've come to see Fenton Hardy, the private investigator."

Frank explained that their father had suddenly been called away on another case. "He asked us to say he's sorry he couldn't wait for you. But he's on a top-secret assignment for the government."

Hammerley looked crestfallen. "That's too bad. I wanted him to handle a case for me. I came all the way from Pennsylvania just to see him."

"Mr. Hammerley, what's your case about?" Joe asked.

"Weather vanes!" Hammerley exclaimed.

The Hardy boys were mystified.

"What have weather vanes got to do with a criminal investigation?" Frank inquired.

"They've been stolen!" Hammerley informed him.

Joe scratched his head. "Who would want to steal weather vanes? And what for?"

Their visitor threw up his hands in astonishment. "Young man, I see you don't understand. These are not ordinary weather vanes. They come from the Pennsylvania Dutch country, where we have them on our houses, barns, churches, and public buildings."

"We have some around Bayport," Joe pointed out.

"I'm sure you do," Hammerley agreed. "But the Pennsylvania Dutch weather vanes are special. Many are large, ornate heirlooms up to two hundred years old. They are immensely valuable as antiques. My neighbor's missing weather vane, the figure of a man on horseback called the *Galloping Rider*, would bring twenty thousand dollars, and more than that if it could be smuggled out of the country. American antiques sell for a king's ransom abroad."

Joe whistled. "Twenty thousand bucks just to tell which way the wind's blowing!"

"That would bring the crooks running," Frank declared.

"Right," Hammerley said. "I represent a group in my county who have lost their valuable weather vanes and want them back!"

"Did you have one stolen yourself?" Frank asked.

The visitor shook his head. "No. My own is still on the barn, and I want it to stay there. It's called the *Flashing Arrow*, an arrow with a two-foot eagle perched on top. The whole thing is of beaten copper. A beautiful work of art! Thieves could sell it for a fortune!"

"But why don't you take it down?" Joe asked. "That way the crooks won't get it."

8

Hammerley gave him a sly look. "I'm setting a trap for the thieves. My foreman sleeps in the barn loft, and he'll sound the alarm if anyone tries to seize the *Flashing Arrow*. So far, nothing has happened. But other people have lost their valuable antiques. I was hoping your father would find them before they disappear into private collections or leave the country."

"How and when were they taken?" Frank asked.

"The thieves who raided my county worked quickly and precisely," the farmer replied. "They struck on four consecutive nights, grabbing the weather vanes before anyone realized what was happening. They knew what they were doing. They took only the most valuable ones."

"How did they get the weather vanes down?" Joe wondered aloud.

"They took the stairs to the roof whenever they could, as in the case of the county courthouse. Then they broke a window and got in while the building was empty. Otherwise, they used ladders to climb up on the outside of buildings. That's how they got the *Galloping Rider*. The police found the marks of the ladder in the mud near the foundation of the barn."

Hammerley sighed, then went on, "Some owners were away at the time, others did not notice at first that their weather vanes were gone from the roofs.

A few angry people who were robbed called the police, and then the story broke on the radio. About twenty were taken. The sheriff and his men inspected every site without finding a clue to the thieves. We're up a tree, so to speak, and there aren't enough officers to stay on the case until it's solved. That's why we need a private investigator."

"Sorry Dad isn't here," Frank said.

"I'm sorry, too," Hammerley confessed. "I was depending on him."

"Maybe he can take your case when he finishes the one he's on," Joe suggested.

Hammerley shook his head vigorously. "Young man, we cannot wait. The trail will grow cold and the thieves will get away. We need a detective right away." He balanced his deerstalker hat on his knee with one hand, tugged on his earlobe, and looked hard at Frank and Joe. "I've heard you boys are detectives, too," he remarked.

"We've worked on several assignments," Joe said modestly, not adding that he and Frank had been involved in more than fifty investigations.

"And you solved them all, I am told," Hammerley commented shrewdly.

"We've got a pretty good batting average," Frank admitted.

Hammerley looked hopeful. "Perhaps you'd be willing to take my case? Judging by your success in the past, I'm sure you could handle it."

Frank pointed out that they would have to check with Mr. Hardy first. "If Dad doesn't need us, it's okay with me."

"Me too!" Joe exclaimed. "I'd like to lasso in the *Galloping Rider* and get it back for you."

"That suits me," Hammerley declared. "How soon can you begin?"

"If we take the case," said Frank, emphasizing the first word, "the timing will depend on our father. He told us to call him tomorrow."

Hammerley brightened up. "Then you could start the day after tomorrow?"

"Maybe," Joe agreed. "How do we get in touch with you?"

Hammerley took a road map of Pennsylvania from his pocket and spread it on the coffee table. "Fly to Lancaster," he said. "Then take Route 222 south to Quarryville. About a mile beyond Quarryville, turn east on a dirt road between two tall pine trees. Keep going for about ten miles, and you will see a sign reading 'Hammerley Homestead.' Drive right on up to the house. I'll be waiting for you."

"You live in the middle of Pennsylvania Dutch country," Frank said with a smile. "That's where people still ride around in buggies drawn by horses, right?"

"That's right," Hammerley said. "Good people, the Amish. We're proud to have them."

The Hardys and their guest chatted for a while

about the Germans who arrived in William Penn's colony back in the eighteenth century. Although Germans, they were called "Dutch" because they referred to themselves with the German word "Deutsch."

"The Pennsylvania Dutch are still there," Hammerley told the boys. "The Amish are the most restrictive group among them. They teach separation from the rest of the world and that you shouldn't go to war, swear oaths, or hold public office. They strive for a simple way of life without modern conveniences and technology."

"I understand they don't even use telephones or electricity on their farms," Joe put in.

Hammerley nodded. "And if someone's property gets damaged, the whole community pitches in and rebuilds it. The barn that belongs to me now was erected in this manner over a century ago."

Hammerley stood up. "I'd better go now. If you want to call me, the number is on my card." Before he walked out the door, he hesitated. "I suppose I should tell you one more thing," he said.

"What's that?" Joe asked eagerly.

The farmer's voice sank to a hoarse whisper. "Beware of the hex!"

2

The Hex

Joe raised his eyebrows in surprise. "The hex?" he repeated. "That's a magical spell, isn't it?"

Hammerley nodded. "That's right. The hex can kill or cure!"

Frank looked puzzled. "Do people still believe in that stuff?"

Hammerley answered him in a stern voice. "The hex may be stronger than you think. Strange things have happened in the Pennsylvania Dutch country, and the local people attribute them to the hex."

"But what has that to do with the stolen weather vanes?" Joe wanted to know.

"There are hex signs on many buildings in our county, including my barn," Hammerley went on.

13

"But the people who lost their weather vanes also lost their hex signs. They believe that the thieves employ a more powerful hex, since they have been so successful. There are also witches who cast spells—white witches who cure illnesses and black witches who harm their victims. Many people feel that the thieves have at least one black witch among them!"

He adjusted his deerstalker hat in a mirror on the wall. "Are you willing to face the hex?" he asked.

Frank and Joe grinned. "I think so," Frank replied.

"Good. I'll be hearing from you then," Hammerley concluded and walked out the door.

Frank and Joe returned to the living room. "Well, brother, what do you think about this hex business?" Joe asked, flopping into an overstuffed chair.

"Let's read up on it," Frank suggested and went into his father's study. He returned with a large, leather-bound tome on mystical lore and found a chapter on the hex. He flattened the book on the coffee table and began to turn the pages, while Joe peered over his shoulder.

They learned that the hex originated in Germany. People believed that hex signs could ward off danger from those who used them. Or, the signs could be applied to focus uncanny forces on victims. German immigrants brought these ideas to America in colonial days, and they have survived to this day in the Pennsylvania Dutch country.

"The owl is the bird of the hex," Frank read, "and talking owls are frequently the pets of witches."

"Talking owls!" Joe marveled. "I wonder what they say."

"To-whitt, to-whoo, the old woodoo," Frank joked. He turned more pages of the book until he reached a plate showing hex signs. Many were geometrical forms in various colors, squares surrounded by a series of triangles, sunbursts inside concentric circles, and so on. The chief hex sign, they learned, was the pentagram, a star pattern of five points that can be drawn without lifting a pencil from a piece of paper.

"We learned how to do that at school and called it a star," Joe said. "But they never told us it was a hex sign."

"Well, it isn't always a hex sign," Frank pointed out. "But when it is, it's a good luck charm, like a rabbit's foot."

"Unless it's being used against you," Joe stated. "That's what the book says. When two people are using the hex, I suppose the winner is the one who's got the toughest witch for a friend."

"Like those weather vane thieves," Frank grumbled and closed the book.

"Hey, what if they steal ours?" Joe said.

"You mean the tin arrow atop our lab over the garage?" Frank grinned. "The one Aunt Gertrude picked up at a tag sale? I'll let you have it for three bucks."

"I'll pass."

Just then the phone rang. "Maybe that's Dad!" Frank exclaimed, jumping to his feet and lifting the instrument from its cradle.

"Is this one of the great Hardys?" a familiar voice inquired.

Frank smiled. "The greatest. What's up, Chet?"

"Arrows!" their friend announced. "I'm getting so good at it I shot ten straight bull's-eyes in a row earlier this morning!"

"You should. After all, you've practiced archery long enough!"

"You really know how to put a guy down," Chet complained. "Even an expert archer doesn't get ten bull's-eyes in a row every day!"

"Okay, okay. Congratulations. Want us to bring you a medal?"

"No, but you could bring yourselves. How about it, Frank? We've got a contest going on here."

Frank conferred briefly with his brother, then promised their pal to be over in fifteen minutes.

Chet Morton, their best friend, was a roly-poly youth who preferred eating to danger. But the Hardys knew he would never let them down if they

16

were in a tight corner. Chet had proved that when he helped them on a number of dangerous investigations.

"Maybe Chet will come up with an idea on those weather vane thefts," Joe said as the brothers drove across Bayport to the farm where their friend lived with his family.

Frank laughed. "You've got to be kidding! All he's interested in is food and his hobbies."

They turned into the driveway to the Morton home and saw a large target with a number of arrows in it on the front lawn near the house. Several of their friends were standing near the gate, watching Chet go through excited motions with his arms and hands.

Frank stopped the car and the boys got out.

"The Hardys have arrived!" Chet announced as the brothers walked toward the group. "Now we can proceed!" He was dressed in dungarees and a corduroy shirt, two buttons of which remained open because his expansive waistline would not permit them to be closed. A quiver was slung across his left shoulder from which protruded the feathered ends of a dozen arrows, and a baseball cap perched jauntily on his head.

Chet obviously relished the role of director of the archery contest. "Go ahead, Phil," he said to the boy next to him. "Let's see what you can do."

Phil Cohen, dark-haired and slender, enjoyed reading as much as sports, even though he was famous for his quickness and agility. He released his arrow with a determined motion. It flew through the air and hit the target in the third ring surrounding the bull's-eye. "Aw, that's not good enough," he grumbled disgustedly.

"Don't worry, you're getting better!" Tony Prito said cheerfully. "A few minutes ago you didn't even hit the target!"

"Thanks, pal," Phil replied, looking at Tony darkly. "Do you have to advertise my mistake? I explained to you that it was only a momentary lack of concentration."

Tony grinned. "Some mistake! You almost killed Biff!"

"He was in my way," Phil said.

Biff Hooper, a husky football player for Bayport High, winced. "I think you did it on purpose, because I ate your sandwich."

Chet interrupted the friendly banter and raised his hand for silence. "We're not here to gab but to learn the skills of archery!" he announced. "Joe, how about trying a shot?"

Joe glanced quickly at Chet's pretty sister Iola, who sat in the grass watching the boys. The vivacious, dark-haired girl was often his date, and he did not want to appear anything less than perfect in front of her.

"Come on, Joe," Tony kidded. "Show Iola what a terrific shot you are!"

Joe shrugged and hefted the bow. He fitted the feathered end of an arrow into the bowstring, took aim, and let loose. He struck the bull's-eye, although not in dead center.

The boys cheered. "Good shot, Joe!"

"Best yet," Tony said.

"The best is yet to come," Chet told him. "The best is me!"

He took his place in the circle occupied by each contestant in turn. Casually, he pushed his cap back on his head, flexed his fingers, and peered across the lawn at the target.

"Ready, Robin Hood?" Frank joshed him.

"Let's see you split Joe's arrow," Iola teased him. "That's what Robin Hood did."

"Don't rush me," Chet said. "This sport needs plenty of concentration." Tightening the bowstring, Chet snapped it until it twanged like the string of a guitar. Then he whipped an arrow over his shoulder from the quiver, with the gesture of an expert showing the amateurs how to do it. Raising the bow, he took aim.

His friends waited expectantly, their eyes glued to the target. Seconds ticked away, but nothing happened.

Then Chet lowered the bow. "Something is wrong with this arrow," he declared.

19

"Oh, no!" Biff groaned.

"Getting nervous?" Tony teased.

"I'll ignore the boos from the gallery," Chet said nonchalantly and picked another arrow from his quiver. Again he took aim as his friends watched in expectant silence.

Chet took his time and shifted his feet to get better balance. Suddenly he hit a slick spot in the ground. He skidded and went over backward, losing his grip on the bow!

Twang-g-g! The string snapped and the arrow lofted high over the Morton house. Chet's yell of dismay was answered by a scream in the backyard.

"The arrow hit somebody!" Joe cried out in alarm. "Come on!" He raced around the house, followed by the others.

3

Trapped in a Tent

There was no one in the backyard but the Mortons' farmhand, Mr. Osborn, who stood at the edge of a pumpkin field. He had his hands on his hips and looked very angry.

When the boys came closer, Mr. Osborn pointed to a big pumpkin neatly pierced by an arrow. "Who did this?" he thundered. "And what's the idea of ruining my vegetables?"

"I—slipped and missed my target," Chet stammered. "But I d-didn't do it on purpose, Mr. Osborn."

The man shook his head in disbelief. "What target? I was weeding around my garden when the arrow flew over here. It could have hit me!"

Chet was crestfallen. "I'm really sorry, Mr. Osborn."

"Tell you what, Chet," Phil suggested diplomatically. "Why don't you finish weeding for Mr. Osborn, and maybe he'll forgive you."

Mr. Osborn seemed more pleased with that idea than Chet. "Well, now, that would be real nice. My back's hurting me anyway. If you do my weeding, I'll take this pumpkin in to Mrs. Osborn and ask her to make a pie. Later you're all invited to have a piece."

Chet's eyes lit up. "It's a deal!" Then he turned to his friends. "You'll help me, won't you?"

To tease Chet, the boys pretended to run away, but then everyone pitched in. While working in Mr. Osborn's garden, the Hardys told the others about Mr. Hammerley and the missing weather vanes. They also mentioned the farmer's antique called the *Flashing Arrow*.

"Sounds like an exciting case!" Chet spoke up. "I'd like to be in on it."

"You should be," Biff said dryly. "You're the expert on arrows!"

"Aw, stop picking on me!" Chet complained.

Frank chuckled. "Don't let it bother you. And if we need help, we'll certainly let you know!"

After breakfast the next morning, the Hardy boys turned on a scrambling device that made it impossible for anyone to listen in on a conversation by tapping their telephone. Joe stood next to his brother so that both could speak to their father, then Frank dialed the number Mr. Hardy had given them. The detective answered at once.

"Oh, I'm glad you called," he said. "I'm on my way out."

"How are things progressing, Dad?" Frank asked.

"So far all right. I'm following a clue that will take me out of town for a while."

"Will you need our help?"

"Not at the moment. Tell me about your meeting with John Hammerley. What did he want?"

Frank described the mystery of the stolen weather vanes, then added, "He wants us to go to his farm tomorrow. If you won't need us in the next few days, is it all right if we take his case?"

"Go ahead," Mr. Hardy said. "But be careful. The gang may be dangerous if so much money's involved. Where can I get in touch with you if I have to?"

Frank gave him Hammerley's number, adding that the farm was close enough to Washington for them to get there in a hurry.

"Fine," Fenton Hardy said. "And good luck on your case."

After their father had hung up, Joe called Mr. Hammerley to say he and Frank would be coming the following day. Hammerley was relieved by the news. "No one has tried to steal the *Flashing Arrow* yet," he reported. "But I'll be glad to have you and your brother on the case."

"Would you mind if we brought a friend along?" Joe asked. "He's helped us on other assignments in the past."

"Of course not. The more the merrier," John Hammerley said with a chuckle.

The following morning, Frank, Joe, and Chet flew from Bayport to Lancaster, where they rented a car. Frank got behind the wheel, with Joe next to him, while Chet climbed in the back. He spread a road map out on his pudgy knees to monitor their way. Soon they were driving along Route 222 through a farming area.

They passed a barn decorated with a green triangle inside a blue square, with straight lines extending out from each of the four corners.

"That's a hex sign," Joe commented.

Chet was suspicious. "What's that mean?"

The Hardys explained the occult geometrical forms used by the Pennsylvania Dutch to ward off evil spirits.

"I don't like it," Chet grumbled. "It's spooky."

"Better get used to it," Frank advised him. "We'll run into more hex signs as we go along."

Recognizing the two tall pine trees mentioned by

Hammerley, Frank turned east on a narrow dirt road flanked by heavy vegetation on both sides. About a mile on, they noticed a cloud of dust approaching.

"Great Scott! It looks like a tornado heading right toward us!" Chet cried out.

"Calm down." Joe grinned. "Tornadoes don't stick to the road."

Frank pulled over into the underbrush. "Let's see what this is all about," he suggested.

The cloud came closer. Finally the boys could make out a line of horses and carriages moving rapidly along in single file. Dust puffed up under the hooves of the animals, who were guided by bearded men dressed in plain farmer's clothing. Beside each driver sat a woman in a long gray dress and an old-fashioned bonnet.

"They're Amish," Frank concluded.

When the caravan came abreast of the car, the men and women waved. The boys waved back. Twelve carriages passed in this manner and vanished down the road.

"They're pretty friendly people," Chet commented. He had scarcely spoken when more sounds of galloping hooves could be heard up the road. A creaking wagon careened through the dust and pulled to a crunching halt next to the car.

Its horse was flecked with foam and tossed its

mane back and forth. The boys stared in astonishment at the driver, a wild-eyed woman whose hair was flying in the wind.

"Are ye natives or outlanders?" she challenged them in a harsh voice.

"Outlanders," Frank replied. "We are from Bayport."

"Then go back," she grated, "or the curse of the hex will get ye! Do nor forget Mad Maggie's warning!"

"Who's Mad Maggie?" Chet asked.

"That's what people call me!" She uttered a screeching laugh, whipped up her horse, and dashed off down the road.

"She must be a local character," Frank guessed.

"She's got the right name," Joe remarked. "She sure looks like Mad Maggie."

Chet mopped his brow with a handkerchief. "She's putting the hex on us. Let's go back to Bayport!"

Frank started the car. "Chet, we promised Mr. Hammerley we wouldn't let the hex scare us."

"*You* did," Chet muttered. "I never promised any such thing!"

Driving on, the boys came to an area where broad fields and meadows extended for miles on either side of the road. Smoke rose into the air from farmhouse chimneys, and farmers were plowing their fields or storing grain in silos next to barns marked by large, multicolored hex signs.

A large tent stood in one field by the side of the road. Stout guy ropes attached to pegs along the sides held it in place, and the canvas roof sloped down from a central high pole that supported it on the inside. People were coming and going through the opening in the front.

A sign over the door proclaimed in large letters:

Joshua Korbo, Auctioneer

Chet spotted a refreshment stand at the side of the tent. "I vote we invest in a hot dog and a bottle of soda!" he spoke up. "What do you say?"

"Okay," Joe agreed, and Frank added, "Sounds like a good idea." He drove to a grassy knoll that served as a temporary parking lot. Leaving the car, the boys strolled over to the stand.

"What's going on?" Joe asked the youth in charge of selling the food.

"Biggest auction of the year in these parts. Folks come from all over the county."

He flipped a hamburger on the grill and began serving another customer.

"Let's stay awhile and watch," Frank suggested. Joe and Chet agreed, and after having their snack, the three walked into the tent. Collapsible chairs were arranged in two groups, about fifty to a group, separated by a narrow aisle. Halfway down the aisle was the tall center pole that kept the tent up. People were milling around, chatting in low voices.

Spotting three unoccupied chairs in the back row, the boys sat down. They had a clear view of the platform where the auctioneer was running his business. He was a medium-sized man, clean shaven, wearing steel-rimmed glasses pushed up on his forehead. A nameplate over his breast pocket identified him as Joshua Korbo.

An assistant carried articles from the back of the tent to the platform, where Korbo offered them to the highest bidder in the audience. There were antiques, china, crystal, paintings, sculptures, and beautiful pieces of jewelry.

"He seems to have enough stuff back there to stock the Bayport Department Store," Chet commented.

"Aunt Gertrude should be here," Joe added. "She loves auctions."

Frank shook his head. "She'd empty her bank account. The price of some of this stuff is far out."

As he spoke, a Colonial silver service went for ten thousand dollars. Next, the assistant placed an antique lamp in front of Korbo, who banged his gavel and started the bidding. People raised their hands to indicate they were interested, and Korbo announced the increasing price as the bids came fast and furious.

"Five hundred, six hundred, seven hundred," the auctioneer called out. "Will anyone bid eight hundred for this valuable lamp? Do I hear eight hundred? Nobody bids eight hundred? Going, going . . ."

Suddenly a fly buzzed past Chet's ear. He swatted at it with his hand.

"Gone!" Korbo boomed. "Sold to the young man in the back row for eight hundred dollars." He pointed his gavel at Chet. "Come forward, sir."

Chet turned pale under his freckles. He seemed mesmerized as Korbo gestured at him sternly with the gavel. Unsteadily Chet rose to his feet and moved up the aisle to the platform. The Hardys followed him.

"Please write out a check for eight hundred dollars," Korbo instructed Chet, "and the lamp is yours."

Chet gulped. "But I didn't bid for it!"

"Of course you did," said Korbo severely. "I saw you raise your hand."

"B-but I was just swatting a fly!" Chet stammered.

"That's right," Frank said. "That's all he did."

An argument started, with Korbo insisting that Chet pay up while the Hardys insisted that the auctioneer had made a mistake. At last the boys convinced Korbo, who disgustedly ordered them to step away from the platform while he got on with the auction.

Relieved that the argument was over, the boys walked toward the back of the tent. Chet mopped his brow. "Thanks for the assist, fellows."

"That's okay," Frank said with a grin. "We only sprung you because we might need you!" As he spoke, he noticed a shadow cast on the wall of the tent by the bright sunlight. Someone was moving along outside, cautiously avoiding the guy ropes attached to the pegs. Frank watched the shadow until it turned the corner and a man appeared in the entrance.

He was a small, wizened figure dressed in the overalls of a farmhand. He sat down near the boys and peered intently at Frank and Joe. Chet had gone ahead and disappeared into the crowd.

Frank nudged Joe. "That guy who just came in seems to be watching us!"

Joe looked at the man out of the corner of his eye. "Why should he? We don't know him from Adam."

Frank shrugged. "I have no idea."

Chet interrupted them by calling out from the back of the tent, where he was standing amid an array of chairs, china, mirrors, rugs, athletic equipment, and other objects. "Boy, we could use this stuff for the Bayport baseball team," he marveled as he pawed through a pile of gloves, masks, and spiked shoes.

The Hardys joined him, forgetting the stranger for a moment. Joe noticed something that caught his attention. Shifting a small table to one side, he lifted the object and examined it. Then he held it up for Frank and Chet to see.

"Look at this!" he exclaimed excitedly.

He was holding a weather vane shaped in the form of a man on horseback. On the base was the descriptive title: *Galloping Rider*.

"It's the stolen weather vane!" Joe surmised.

"Sure looks like it," Frank stated. "What'll we do now?"

"Let's bid for it," Joe proposed.

"Not me!" Chet retorted. "I'm not bidding for anything. Not even a hot dog."

Before they could work out a strategy, they heard footsteps coming in their direction. They turned and saw the stranger in overalls, who had bounded out of his chair and was plunging toward them in a headlong attack!

The man barreled into Joe, wrenching the weather vane from his hands and knocking him over backward. The Hardy boy fell against his brother and both went down in a heap. Chet got a bear hug on their assailant, but the latter twisted around, hit him on the head with the weather vane, and made him see stars.

Breaking loose, the man bolted up the aisle carrying the weather vane. He elbowed his way through the crowd and hastened toward the exit.

"Stop thief!" Joe yelled. "Don't let him get away!"

Realizing that no one could make out what was happening, the Hardys leaped to their feet and dashed after the fugitive, with Chet close behind them. Frantically they tried to push their way through the bidders in the aisle.

Striving to get around one group, Chet stumbled and crashed into the tent pole, knocking it loose. The tent swayed crazily for a moment, then started to collapse!

4

Vanishing Weather Vanes

Cries went up from the crowd as the tent fell down like a cloud, enveloping everyone in its folds.

"Let me out!" a woman screamed.

"We'll be smothered!" someone else yelled over the excited shouts of other people.

Frank pushed up the limp cloth over his head and looked around for Joe and Chet. They were right next to him.

"Come on, let's try to crawl out of here," he urged and began to scramble forward on his hands and knees. The other two followed. Reaching the side of the tent, they wriggled underneath, loosened a guy rope by releasing it from its peg, and lifted the canvas above their heads.

"This way, everybody!" Frank shouted.

Those trapped in the tent struggled clear, aided by the boys from Bayport.

"Good thinking!" one man complimented them.

"I believe no one was hurt thanks to you," said another.

Korbo, who had been on the auctioneer's platform when the tent collapsed, was the last to escape. He railed furiously at Chet's clumsiness in barging into the pole.

"What Chet did wasn't as bad as auctioning stolen property!" Frank interjected.

"Everything that I handle is legitimate!" Korbo snapped.

"What about that weather vane called the *Galloping Rider?*"

"There were no weather vanes at this auction. Look for yourself." Korbo took a list from his pocket and handed it to Frank, who checked the "W" entries.

"Wagon, warming pan, washing machine, wheelbarrow, writing desk," Frank read. "No weather vane. I guess we owe you an apology, Mr. Korbo."

"But the weather vane was in the tent!" Joe protested. He explained how he had found it and how the stranger had snatched it away from him.

"I don't know anything about a weather vane or that man you're talking about," Korbo said, "but I do know who knocked the tent down." He pointed an accusing finger at Chet, who turned red with embarrassment.

"We'll put it up again," Frank offered. Korbo accepted the suggestion with a curt nod, and the boys set to work.

Wriggling back under the canvas, they reached the center of the tent, where they found the pole tilted at an angle but still attached to the roof. They took hold of the support, straining to get enough leverage, then gradually eased it into an upright position and wedged the base against the ground where it had been. Then, with the help of some other young people, they righted the chairs and tightened the guy ropes outside.

The auction resumed while the Bayporters drove on toward the Hammerley farm.

"Maybe that guy stole the weather vane and hid it in the tent for some reason," Joe observed. "He might have come back to pick it up on the sly, but we got there first."

"That would explain why it was stashed behind the table," Frank agreed.

A sign loomed ahead of them in the distance:

HAMMERLEY HOMESTEAD

Frank turned a few feet beyond it and drove toward the big house. A barn with a tall silo attached to it stood behind the place, and moving in the wind atop the barn was the copper-colored figure of an eagle perched on an arrow.

"The *Flashing Arrow!*" Joe pointed.

Frank nodded. "And it's up to us to see it stays where it is." He parked in front of the house and the three went up to the front door. Chet punched the bell. Hammerley appeared and smiled happily when he saw his callers. Frank introduced Chet as the friend who would be on the case with them.

Hammerley was pleased. "An extra member always strengthens the team," he said. He was surprised when Joe told him about the *Galloping Rider.* "You mean the thieves were about to auction it off?" the farmer thundered.

"Mr. Korbo didn't even have it on his list," Frank explained. "He didn't know how it got there or who took it."

Hammerley sighed. "Too bad you couldn't catch the man who ran off with it. Well, let's go over to the barn and I'll show you my prized possession on the roof."

He led the way through the yard. The boys saw hired hands dumping corn from a truck onto a conveyor belt leading into the silo. Some distance away, a line of horses looking out from their stalls indicated the building where the livestock were kept. Chickens clucked in a coop nearby, and a hawk wheeled in the sky overhead.

Hammerley stopped in front of the barn. "This is where I keep the hay, feed, and farm implements," he informed his visitors.

Looking up, the boys saw a hex sign over the front door. It was a bright red pentagram in a white square, which was inside a black circle.

"The original owner put the hex sign there to protect the barn," Hammerley explained.

"Wouldn't it also protect the *Flashing Arrow?*" Frank queried.

Hammerley scowled. "Maybe, but some hexes are stronger than others, and I'm not taking any chances. The thieves might be using the pentagram hex too. Now follow me."

He led them around the barn, explaining that, because of its height, anyone climbing up to the roof would have to use a fireman's ladder. "There's a staircase inside. It leads to that skylight above the gutter, which is the only exit from the loft to the roof."

The boys craned their necks to see where he was pointing. They noticed a man glaring down at them from the skylight with a sinister expression. He pulled back when he saw them looking at him.

"I wouldn't want to meet him in a dark alley," Chet muttered.

"Cheer up," Joe encouraged their rotund friend. "No alleys on the farm."

"Very funny!" Chet growled.

38

The group circled the barn and arrived back at the front door. "You can see how the other weather vanes vanished," Hammerley noted. "They were left unprotected. Here, as long as somebody is in the loft, the *Flashing Arrow* is safe. My foreman has been sleeping in the barn for the past few nights, as I told you in Bayport."

Just then the man they had seen at the skylight came out of the door. Hammerley introduced him as Crow Morven, the foreman of the farm.

"I was in the loft all night," Morven reported to Hammerley. "Nothing happened. I guess the crooks aren't thinking of stealing your weather vane."

"Could be a setup," Chet said. "Make you forget the *Flashing Arrow's* in danger, and one night— whammo—it'll be gone."

"You got it figured out, haven't you, wise guy?" Morven scoffed. "The *Flashing Arrow* is safe as long as I'm foreman. You can bet on it."

"Nobody's betting against you, Crow," Hammerley soothed his employee. "Now, suppose you take our visitors up to the roof and let them inspect the weather vane."

The farmer went back to the house, while Morven led the way into the barn. They climbed the stairs past two landings into the loft, which was a broad room with a low ceiling. A pile of hay filled one corner. The skylight window admitted the rays of the sun.

Morven pushed open the skylight, allowing the boys to see how the roof dropped away at a steep angle toward the gutter. There was nothing beneath it but a long fall down to the ground.

The foreman gave the boys an evil grin. "Want to follow me out there?" he challenged them.

"Sure," said Frank and Joe.

Chet poked his head out the skylight, blanched at the height, and quickly pulled back. "I think I'll pass," he gasped. "I'll check out the loft instead."

Frank and Joe climbed through the skylight after the unfriendly foreman, pressing their feet against the gutter to get a toehold. Then, doubled over and clutching the wooden shingles with their fingers as they went, they worked their way up the steep incline of the roof.

Although Morven was used to the barn, he fell behind Frank and Joe in the climb to the apex, where the other side of the roof dropped away in the opposite direction. Joe was in the lead. Halfway up, a shingle snapped in his hand, but he managed to steady himself.

When they reached the apex, they stood up. They could see the surrounding area. A stream meandered through a woods, and a row of small hills rose beyond it.

"Time to go back," Morven said after they had taken in the view. "I haven't got all day!"

"We'd like to inspect the weather vane first," Frank replied. "Mr. Hammerley said we should."

"Is there some reason you don't want us near it?" Joe asked suspiciously.

"Of course not," Morven snarled. "Come on."

The Hardys were used to heights. They had done some mountaineering, and many of their cases had forced them into death-defying feats high above the ground. But both felt rather uneasy on the roof of Hammerley's barn.

To reach the weather vane, they had to crouch on their hands and knees, then edge their way along the apex, with disaster on either side should they slip. Finally the trio reached the middle of the roof, and the Hardys had a close-up view of the *Flashing Arrow*.

A Pennsylvania Dutch craftsman had beaten flat copper into the likeness of an eagle with its head back in a defiant gesture, its beak open as if to attack, and its wings spread for flight. The eagle's talons gripped the arrow on which it perched. One end of the arrow was pointed, while the other end expanded into simulated feathers. A bar through the center of the arrow held the weather vane in place on the roof.

Frank and Joe edged their way around Morven and sat on opposite sides of the *Flashing Arrow* so that they could inspect it together. They were struck by the beauty of the workmanship.

"Look, it's loose," Frank said, lifting the weather vane from its bar. "How come?"

Morven shrugged. "Beats me. It had a collar that held it on the bar."

"Where's the collar now?"

"Search me," Morven said. "Maybe the workmen who fixed the roof took it."

Frank replaced the weather vane on the bar, noting that it could still turn in the wind without falling off. Joe swung it around until the arrow pointed in his direction. He wiggled to sit next to Morven, with his legs dangling down one side of the roof, and explored the pointed end with his fingertips.

"Say, this arrowhead isn't welded on," he said. "It's screwed on." Grasping the arrowhead between his thumb and forefinger, he gave it a sharp twist that caused it to move.

"Let's see," Morven said. He rose and leaned toward Joe. Just then his foot seemed to slip and he fell heavily against the young detective. With a cry of surprise, he righted himself with his hand, but Joe was knocked off balance and toppled from the apex of the roof.

While Frank stared in horror, his brother slid down the steep slope and plunged over the side of the barn!

5

Joe's Close Call

Without hesitating, Frank skidded down the roof to a point where he could brace his feet against the gutter. Joe was hanging onto the gutter by his fingertips! The force of his fall had swung one foot against the wall, where the sole of his shoe had come to rest on a fastening that held a drainpipe against the side of the barn.

Quickly Frank grabbed his brother's wrists. Joe swung one knee over the gutter and with Frank's help hauled himself back onto the roof. He lay there for a moment, breathing heavily after his near-fatal accident.

"That was some ride you took," Frank said, his voice still tense.

"I'm glad I didn't finish it," Joe puffed. Catching his breath, he followed Frank back to the apex of the roof where Morven was waiting.

"I'm sorry about your fall," the foreman said apologetically. "My foot slipped. Are you all right?"

"Don't worry, I do this all the time," Joe said coldly. He suspected that it had not been an accident. Carefully wedging himself next to the weather vane, he resumed unscrewing the arrowhead and noticed that the arrow formed a hollow tube.

"That makes it light enough to turn with the wind," he reasoned. After peering in and finding the tube empty, he screwed the arrowhead back on.

Deciding that they had seen enough, Frank and Joe descended the roof with Morven, dropped through the skylight, and rejoined Chet in the loft. Their roly-poly friend, who had watched Joe's close call, was pale, and his hands trembled slightly.

"You sure know how to scare a guy," he said to Joe, trying not to show how upset he was.

"Sorry about that," Joe said. "I didn't know you were watching. What'd you find in the loft?"

"Nothing but a telephone," Chet replied and pointed to the instrument that was mounted on the wall. "I checked it out. Connects with the house. Matter of fact, Mr. Hammerley wants you to call him up."

Frank lifted the phone and heard it ring at the other end. Hammerley answered.

"Did you find anything?" he inquired.

"Yes. The *Flashing Arrow* is loose. I lifted it clear off its rod. Why is that?"

Hammerley was puzzled. "I don't know. It always had a collar holding it in place. I'll talk to Crow about it. Tell him to come to the house with you."

The group entered through the front door and Hammerley ushered them into the living room. He ordered Morven to put a new collar on the weather vane, and the foreman promised to take care of it in the morning.

"What's our next move?" Harmmerley asked the boys.

"Tomorrow we'd like to talk to the people whose weather vanes have been stolen," Frank said. "Meanwhile, perhaps we could sleep in the barn tonight. I'm sure Mr. Morven wouldn't mind having some time off."

Hammerley liked the idea, and Morven gave no indication that he objected in any way. He took a flashlight from a shelf on the wall, stuffed it into his pocket, and said he would see about the cows in the pasture. As he was leaving, he turned to the boys with a smirk and added, "Pleasant dreams!"

Hammerley showed his guests around the house,

then entertained them with tales of the Pennsylvania Dutch and the plain ways of the Amish. He was interested to hear that they had seen Amish couples in their carriages on their way.

"We also met Mad Maggie," Frank said but did not mention the woman's warning.

"Oh, she's a harmless old crone," Hammerley told the boys. "No one takes her seriously."

Frank decided not to press the subject any further, when Chet suddenly sat bolt upright. His eyes became wide, and his nose quivered.

"What's the matter, Chet?" Frank asked.

"Food!" Chet exclaimed. "I smell it! And I just remembered that we haven't eaten in a long time!"

The familiar aroma of roast beef wafted in from the kitchen, and the Hardys grinned.

"Mr. Hammerley, please excuse Chet," Frank said. "He has this thing about food—"

"I can tell." Hammerley chuckled. "And I assure you he'll enjoy tonight's meal."

An hour later their host served onion soup from a large green tureen at the head of the table. The roast beef came next, with vegetables and potatoes, and finally Mrs. Smith, the housekeeper, brought in homemade ice cream. Chet took a double portion of everything.

Hammerley was amazed at the spectacle. "My

goodness, young man, you really know how to do justice to a meal!" he commented.

"Chet's had a lot of practice," Joe stated.

Later, as night was falling, the boys left the house and went to the barn. They climbed up to the loft and discussed their strategy. They agreed to rotate one-hour watches—Joe first, Chet second, Frank third, and then back to Joe to repeat the series.

Then they went to the skylight and peered out. Dark clouds drifted across the face of a full moon, causing the trees in the woods to throw ghostly shadows over the landscape. From down below came the scream of a wildcat hunting for its prey in the underbrush. Bats flitted in the night sky, zooming through the moonlight and disappearing into the darkness. Far off, a bell tolled mournfully in a church steeple.

"Let's keep the light out," Frank suggested and sat down. "It might scare the thieves away."

"But I'm scared without it!" Chet declared. "This place gives me the creeps."

"Want to sleep in the farmhouse?" Frank needled.

Chet looked at him darkly but didn't reply. Finally he said, "What if the thieves outnumber us?"

"We have a phone to send an SOS," Frank told him. "Besides, the hex is on our side."

Being reminded of the hex sign over the barn door made Chet feel more uneasy than ever. Frank and Joe could not help but tease their pal, and they began to discuss how witches used hex signs to cast spells on their victims.

"Strange things happen at the crossroads in the dark of the moon," Joe intoned. It was a sentence he had read in the book on mystical lore.

Chet shivered. "Please, fellows, let's talk about something else. The only thing I want is—"

His companions never found out what he wanted because he was interrupted by a sound on the roof in the vicinity of the weather vane. They jumped to their feet and quickly opened the skylight. They were about to climb out onto the roof, when they realized what had made the noise.

A large horned owl sat on the arrow beside the copper eagle. It glared at them, hooted hoarsely, spread its wings, and sailed off into the moonlight.

Frank and Joe broke out into relieved chuckles. "Some thief!" Joe said.

"It certainly didn't do my nerves any good," Chet grumbled, wiping perspiration from his face.

The three settled down again to wait in the darkness. Chet yawned. He kicked some of the hay in the corner into a makeshift mattress. "I'm going to sleep," he announced and lay down. He closed his eyes and soon only his snoring disturbed the silence of the barn loft.

Joe glanced at the luminous dial of his wristwatch. "Time for me to stand guard, Frank. You can turn in if you want to."

"Good idea," Frank said. "I could use a little shut-eye."

But before he could get comfortable, a creaking noise came from downstairs. "Sh!" Frank warned, putting a hand on Joe's right arm. The Hardys sat motionless, straining their ears.

"It must have been the door," Joe whispered. "Maybe the wind did it." But then they heard a step creak on the lower stairs, then another, and another!

"That's not the wind," Frank hissed. "Someone's coming up the stairs!"

In their detective work, the boys had developed a technique for dealing with situations like this. Noiselessly they tiptoed to the door and positioned themselves on either side of it.

The stealthy footsteps drew closer and stopped on the landing outside. Frank and Joe felt their spines tingle and they breathed in muted gasps, while their eyes remained fixed on the door.

It began to swing inward very slowly, inch by inch. When it was half open, a dark form slipped through into the loft! The Hardys could see the intruder was a man but did not recognize him. They sprang into action. Joe grabbed the stranger by the elbows, pulling his arms behind his back, while Frank got him around the waist.

49

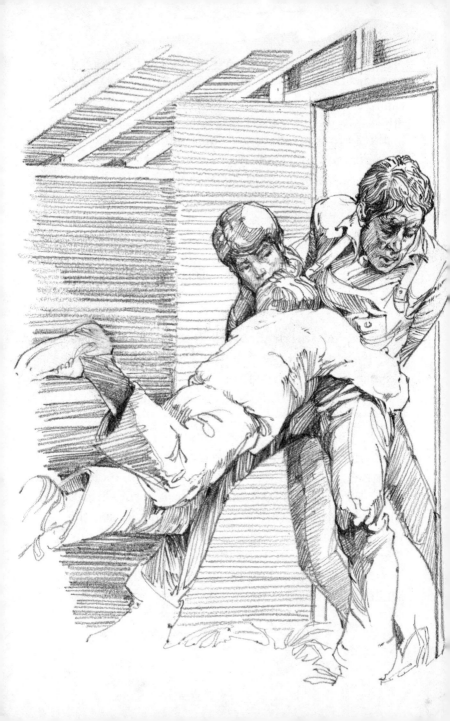

However, their adversary was quick and strong. He wrenched free of Joe's grip and jumped clear of Frank. Then he bolted out the door! Frank hit him with a flying tackle, and the two rolled over and over down the stairs to the landing below.

The kicking and pounding had awakened Chet. He and Joe rushed down the stairs after the two combatants to join the fray. Seconds later Chet immobilized the intruder with a headlock!

6

Helicopter Caper

"All right, I give up!" the captive sputtered. "Just let go of me!"

The voice sounded familiar to the boys, so they quickly pushed the intruder up the steps and into the loft where they shone the light on him. He was Crow Morven!

"What in the world are you doing here?" Frank exploded.

"I came for my jacket," the man replied. "I must have left it in the loft."

"But why did you sneak up the stairs?" Joe demanded. "Why didn't you just call out and let us know you were here?"

"I figured you were asleep, and I didn't want to

wake you up. Did you have to pounce on me like that?"

"You threw a few punches yourself," Chet accused him. "And if you'd let us know who you were in the beginning, we all could have saved ourselves a lot of bruises!"

"I know," Morven muttered. "But after you jumped me I wasn't sure whether it was you or the gang of thieves. After all, they could have come in and subdued you. Anyway, have you seen my jacket?"

"You were wearing it over at the house," Joe reminded him. "I saw you put the flashlight in your pocket."

"Oh . . . yes. Now I remember. I must have left it out in the pasture," Morven said, slapping his forehead with his hand. "Well, sorry about the bruises. I'll see you in the morning." With that, he turned on his heels and left.

Joe snapped the light off again. "I don't trust that guy," he declared. "He didn't forget his jacket. He was up to no good when he came sneaking in here!"

"And remember how he tried to keep us away from the *Flashing Arrow*?" Frank asked. "Why would he do that if he was on the level? Maybe *he* took the collar off and didn't want us to find out."

Chet nodded. "Joe, when he bumped into you, it

53

wasn't an accident, either. He was probably trying to knock you off the roof."

"I felt that all along," Joe admitted.

The boys agreed to keep an eye on Morven. After the excitement of the fight, none of them felt like sleeping. It occurred to Frank that it would be a good idea to check out the rest of the barn. "Morven could have dropped something downstairs before coming up," he said. "One of us can stay here while the other two investigate."

They decided that Joe would remain on guard while Frank and Chet scouted through the lower levels. Frank took out his pencil flashlight. Using its narrow beam, he led the way down the stairs.

At the bottom, they found a dozen stone steps, descended them, and ended up in a basement constructed from large cinder blocks. Chet yelled as something jumped onto his shoe. Frank whipped the flashlight around and the beam picked up a rat scurrying out of sight.

Pressing on, the boys discovered farm machinery and a long bench holding tools for working on the machines.

"This must be the repair shop," Frank judged.

Chet slapped a tractor with the palm of his hand. "Boy, I'd like to drive this baby out in the field! I'd show them how to make furrows!"

He got into the driver's seat of the tractor and

began to experiment with the controls in the darkness, while Frank played his light on the ceiling.

Varrooom! Suddenly the tractor engine sprang to life and the machine began to move, plowing forward into a pile of crates before Chet managed to brake to a halt! It all happened so fast that Frank could only stare at his friend, who was now festooned with straw that had fallen over him from one crate. The pile tilted at crazy angles over his head, and Chet looked horror-stricken at a broken crate in front of him.

"I just turned on the ignition, and it took off!" he declared defensively.

"You must have kicked it into gear without noticing it," Frank said, suppressing a chuckle.

"I guess so." Chet backed the tractor to its original position and jumped down to inspect the crates he had hit. "Only one is smashed," he said with relief.

"They can use it for kindling," Frank encouraged him.

Chet pushed his hand through his hair to remove the straw and ran a finger around his collar. Then the two boys continued around the basement in the darkness. The flashlight showed dust and cobwebs everywhere except over one cinder block, where the mortar around the block had been pried loose and removed.

"This looks like a hiding place!" Frank exclaimed excitedly. "Let's see what's in it."

Together they shifted the block back and forth and drew it from its position in the wall. Frank shone his beam into the cavity. They saw a parcel wrapped in brown paper inside.

"Maybe it's a bomb!" Chet said in alarm.

"I won't take any chances," Frank promised. Picking up a long, thin stick from the floor, he stood to one side of the cavity and prodded the brown paper off the parcel. Underneath was a white cube about six inches square on each side.

"That's no bomb," Frank muttered. Reaching in, he lifted the cube out, examined it, and began to chuckle. The whiteness was the reflection of waxed paper. Removing it, he held up a couple of sandwiches.

"One of the farmhands must have put it behind the cinder block to keep the rats away," Frank surmised.

He put the sandwiches back in the paper covering, replaced them in their hiding place, and with Chet's help pushed the cinder block into its old position. Then the boys proceeded toward the rear door of the barn, where the machinery entered and left. It was locked. Slowly, they continued along the wall and finally arrived back at the steps.

"Let's go up to the next level," Frank suggested.

"I don't think there are any clues down here."

Chet nodded, and they climbed the stone staircase to examine the ground floor. This part of the barn was used for storing grain. Frank and Chet shuffled forward cautiously, passing bins of wheat, oats, rye, and corn.

At the end of the row of bins, Frank turned right in the darkness, guided by the narrow beam of his flashlight. Chet, who was behind him, had caught his sleeve on a nail, which held him up for a moment. When he reached the place where Frank had turned, the light was too far away for him to see. He went left, expecting to catch up with his friend. Suddenly something clapped him on the shoulder, making him stop in paralyzed fright.

"Is th-that you, Frank?" Chet whispered tremulously.

There was no answer. He reached up and felt a soft pressure inside burlap sacking. The truth dawned on him. The corner of a large sack of grain had shifted under its own weight, sloped over as he passed, and struck him on the shoulder!

Running the back of his hand across his forehead, Chet hurried on until he saw a dim light in the wall of the barn. He figured it must be the open door to another room and that Frank was in there. Quickly he stepped through and, with a terrified scream, plunged into darkness! He landed on a pile of corn in the silo.

Groggily he struggled to his feet and discovered that the aperture of the silo was too high for him to climb through. "Frank!" he yelled. "Frank, help me!"

The older Hardy boy, having circled the room, was near enough to hear Chet shouting. Hastening to the spot, he shone his light down into the silo. Chet stood there, ankle-deep in corncobs. His mouth was open and his eyes were glazed.

"Chet, are you inspecting the corn for the horses and cows?" Frank asked with a chuckle.

"Just get me out of here!" Chet pleaded.

Frank spotted a rope on a hook and lowered one end to his friend. Then he wound the opposite end around a pulley used in lifting heavy sacks of grain and helped Chet scramble out.

"I've had it!" Chet declared emphatically. "I want to get out of here pronto!"

"We haven't finished investigating," Frank pointed out. "There's the second floor—"

"Oh, all right," Chet grumbled. "But don't lose me again!"

They ascended the stairs to the next level of the barn. Here they made a rapid inspection of lighter farm implements—shovels, hoes, rakes, crowbars, pruning hooks, and so on.

"Nothing here either," Frank said finally. "Let's get back to the loft and see what Joe's doing."

But when the two arrived, Joe was gone!

"Where in the world is he?" Frank said worriedly as he put on the light and looked around the loft. "He wouldn't leave without letting us know!"

"Maybe the thieves got to him while we were gone," Chet said nervously.

"It's possible," Frank replied somberly. "We were in the basement long enough that they could have hustled him down the stairs without our knowing it! If so, I'd better get on their trail. You stay here, Chet, while I run outside and see if I can find out what happened!"

Frank was heading for the door when a dark shape loomed on the roof against the rising moon. The figure raised its arm as if to spring through the skylight!

"Frank!" Chet quavered. "Don't go!"

Frank turned. "What's up?"

Speechlessly Chet pointed to the dark shape on the roof. As they stared, the figure swung down through the skylight into the loft. It was Joe!

"I thought that owl we spotted might have knocked the weather vane off center," he said. "So I went out to see before it tumbled down to the ground. What a windfall for the crooks that would have been! Did you find anything downstairs?"

"Nothing," Frank reported. "Chet even checked out the silo."

Their rotund pal squirmed as Frank described the incident to Joe. "Knock it off, fellows, will you?" Chet pleaded.

"Don't worry, we know we can count on you," Frank mollified him. "And now it's your turn to stand guard."

Chet parked himself on the floor with his back to the wall, while the Hardys lay down to sleep. Squinting through the skylight, he could see dismal clouds scudding across the moon. A rising wind shook the shingles of the roof with a mournful sound. Chet shuddered and felt relieved that he was not alone in the darkness of the barn loft.

The minutes slipped away slowly. Everything was still, and Chet began to nod. Soon a snore arose from his corner. Fast asleep, he did not hear a faint sound in the night sky that grew louder as it approached.

Suddenly a terrific clatter erupted overhead, waking the three boys. The noise continued past the barn, started to die away, then came back with a thunderous roar that shook the building.

Frank and Joe leaped to their feet and rushed over to the skylight. Chet dived under the pile of hay. The noise diminished once more, and the Hardys climbed onto the roof. In the moonlight, they could see a helicopter circling for another approach to the barn. Again the clatter became deafening.

"What's that chopper doing?" Frank shouted in consternation over the noise.

"I don't know!" Joe yelled back. "The pilot must be a complete fool! He'll hit the barn!"

The helicopter came directly toward them. Someone on the inside played out a cable on a winch. It dropped ten feet and swayed back and forth under the chopper, which hovered over the roof. Four curved prongs spread out at the end of the cable.

"He's got a grappling hook at the end!" Frank shouted. "They're after the *Flashing Arrow!*"

The chopper moved slightly and the cable swung toward the weather vane. Then the grappling iron struck the copper eagle with a loud clang. It missed. The whirlybird passed over the barn with only feet to spare, flew off far enough to circle around, then started back toward the weather vane, lower than ever. Joe could see the painted legend on its side: JF333.

The boys were scrambling up the roof in a frantic effort to reach the weather vane first. At the apex, they edged their way along the route they had taken with Morven during the day. It was even more dangerous in the darkness, but the boys gritted their teeth and pressed on as fast as they could, with Frank in the lead.

As he approached the *Flashing Arrow,* the chopper came directly toward him. It was so near that he could see the face of the pilot at the window, but the darkness prevented him from distinguishing his features.

Frank had almost reached the weather vane when the grappling iron swung toward it from the opposite side. The metal claws closed beneath the arrow of the weather vane and grabbed it as the man at the winch jerked the cable upward!

Desperately Frank lunged forward, his arm outstretched and his fingers grasping for the weather vane. But he missed by inches as the grappling hook plucked the *Flashing Arrow* from its bar. The winch rolled in the cable, drawing its prey into the interior of the chopper.

Then the helicopter moved up and disappeared into the darkness!

7

The Charging Bull

Frank slumped over the apex, breathing heavily. Joe almost lost his balance from the wind caused by the chopper's blades, and for a few moments the brothers rested in silence. Then they made their way back to the loft.

"I hate to tell Mr. Hammerley what happened," Frank muttered.

"I know," Joe said. "But we have no choice." He lifted the phone and listened. Then he jiggled the instrument. "It's dead!" he declared.

Frank walked to the skylight and hauled in the wire. "It's been cut. Judging by the length, it was severed down below. I'll go over to Mr. Hammerley and tell him. You and Chet might just as well stay here."

He left the barn and walked to the house, where he pressed the doorbell. Getting no response, he pushed the bell several more times. Then he banged the knocker and hammered on the door with his fist, at the same time shouting, "Mr. Hammerley! Mr. Hammerley!" Still, no answer came from inside the house.

Frank walked around the building knocking on the windows and at the back door, all to no avail. He was wondering what to do next when out of the corner of his eye he noticed a movement in the underbrush flanking the woods. A man was sneaking away!

Frank called out for him to stop, but the stranger started to run. Guiding himself by the sound of crashing through the underbrush, Frank ran after him. He caught up with the fugitive about twenty yards into the woods. Panting for breath, the man swung around, and his face became visible in the beam of Frank's flashlight.

He was Crow Morven!

"What were you doing hiding in the bushes?" Frank demanded.

"I was on my way home. When I saw you sneaking around the house, I thought you were a burglar, so I watched you."

"Didn't you hear me call Mr. Hammerley and recognize my voice?" Frank asked.

Morven shook his head, pulling loose of Frank's grip. The young detective realized he had no right to stop the foreman, so he let him go and watched him disappear into the woods. Then he returned to the loft. Dawn was just breaking.

"Morven's our prime suspect," Joe said after hearing Frank's tale.

His brother agreed. "Unfortunately, we still don't have any proof."

The boys decided there was no point in remaining in the loft, now that the weather vane was gone. They moved to the front porch of the house and sat on wicker chairs around a small table until the housekeeper arrived at 8:00 A.M. She let them in with her key, saying she was surprised that Mr. Hammerley was still in bed. "He's always up when I get here," she added, shaking her head. She went upstairs, calling the farmer.

At last he appeared, breathing slowly and with his face flushed. Yawning drowsily he invited the boys to have breakfast with him. "Anything exciting happen during the night?" he asked.

"I'm afraid so," Frank said hesitantly. "The *Flashing Arrow* was stolen!"

"What!" Hammerley exploded.

Frank explained how the thieves had managed to remove the weather vane, and he watched Hammerley's angry face with apprehension.

"You knew the thieves might try to steal my antique. Why did you let them take it from under your noses?" the farmer thundered.

"We didn't expect a chopper," Chet pointed out. "Neither did you."

Hammerley simmered down. "You have a point there, young man. This is the first time I ever heard of robbery by helicopter." He frowned thoughtfully, then sat down at the table. "So the crooks changed their method of operation. Is my hex sign still there?"

"It's there," Joe confirmed. "They had no chance to take it."

"We tried to phone you after it happened," Frank said, "but the line was cut." He explained how he had attempted to deliver the message in person, only to find complete silence at the house.

"I can't understand why I didn't hear you," the farmer said. "I'm usually a light sleeper. But I didn't hear the helicopter you described, either. And I overslept this morning. Couldn't seem to wake up when Mrs. Smith called me. It's mystifying."

"Not if you were slipped a drug," Frank declared. He looked closely at the farmer. "You were breathing rather slowly when you came down, and your face was red," he added. "Those are symptoms of chloral mixed with alcohol. Did you take anything before you went to sleep last night?"

"Only my nighttime cocoa."

"Where's the cup?"

"It was on my bedside table. Mrs. Smith may have taken it to the kitchen by now."

"We'd like to see it before she washes it."

Hammerley led the way into the kitchen. The housekeeper was just about to put the cup into the sink.

"Hold it, Mrs. Smith!" Joe called. "May we have that cup for a moment?"

She handed it to the boy. At the bottom were the crusted remains of the cocoa Hammerley had drunk the night before.

"I'll get the kit," Joe offered and went upstairs to the room where they had left their bags. Soon he returned with a small detective box the boys always carried with them on their trips. He set it on the kitchen table and removed an eyedropper with a chemical in it. He added a few drops of water from the faucet, then squeezed the solution onto the caked remains of the cup. Transparent crystals formed at the bottom.

"That's chloral hydrate!" Joe declared. "Mr. Hammerley, you *were* drugged!"

"Seems like a strong dose," Frank added. "Who made your cocoa last night?"

"Mrs. Smith, as usual," Hammerley replied.

The housekeeper's face went ashen. "I didn't put

anything in Mr. Hammerley's cocoa!" she cried out.

Chet put an arm around the excited woman's shoulder. "No one's accusing you," he said, trying to calm her.

"Let's test the can of cocoa," Frank suggested. He tried the same experiment and discovered there were knockout drops in the can, too. "That means anyone who had access to the can during the day could have done it," he concluded.

"It must have been yesterday," Hammerley stated. "I had cocoa from that can the night before last, and it was perfectly all right then."

"Can you remember who came to your house yesterday?" Joe prodded.

Hammerley frowned. "The usual tradesmen, some grain dealers from Lancaster, and a couple of politicians who want me to run for the town council in the next election."

"Crow Morven was here," Chet pointed out.

"Yes, but only in the front room," Hammerley replied. "He wasn't in the kitchen."

"He could have sneaked in while no one was looking," Joe suggested.

"Morven wouldn't do a thing like that!" Hammerley defended his foreman. "I trust him."

"He sneaked into the barn last night," Joe reminded the farmer. "And he was hiding in the bushes after the helicopter took off."

Hammerley shrugged. "He thought he left his

jacket. And later he told you he was on his way home. He stays up until that time quite often, checking around the property to see that everything is all right."

Frank signaled Joe not to press the matter any further. Apparently Hammerley trusted his foreman, and they would need proof to convince him of any wrongdoing on Morven's part.

Just then the foreman walked into the house. When he heard what had happened, he jeered at the boys. "You guys are a great bunch of detectives! Fooled by a copter."

He urged Hammerley to fire the young sleuths, since they had not been able to prevent the theft.

"After all," he insisted, "the weather vane was safe while I was on guard in the barn!"

"Maybe you know more about the chopper than we do!" Chet challenged him.

Morven glared at Frank. "I was on the ground when the chopper came overhead. You saw me. Remember?"

"Correct," Frank admitted.

Hammerley intervened in the dispute. "The question is, what to do now?"

"We lost the *Flashing Arrow*," Joe stated. "But we're determined to find it and bring it back!"

"Where will you begin?" Hammerley asked doubtfully.

"We have a clue. I saw the license number on the

chopper—JF333. Have you any idea what that could mean?"

"It probably means the helicopter came from Juniper Field," Hammerley said. "That's a small airport five miles from here. Why don't you drive over there and check it out?"

"No use driving," Morven advised. "The bridge up the road was washed out by the last flood. Hasn't been repaired yet. The detour will take you fifty miles around the hills. It's five miles to walk."

"Which direction?" Joe inquired.

"Across the pasture to the big maple tree on the other side. Follow the footpath between two big boulders and it'll lead you to Juniper Field." Saying he had some farm chores to look after, the foreman left the house.

"We'll walk, then," Joe decided. "Okay with you fellows?"

Frank agreed at once, but Chet hesitated. The idea of a five-mile hike did not appeal to him. But he did not want to be left out of the investigation, so he set out with Frank and Joe for Juniper Field.

As they passed the barn, they saw Morven looking at them from the skylight. He had a grim smile on his face and he shook his fist at them.

"That guy knows more than he lets on," Frank thought to himself. "We'll have to watch him very closely."

The three boys crossed the Hammerley farm between plowed fields and reached a barbed wire fence where the pasture began. Next to the gate stood a pen made of heavy boards. A gigantic bull in the pen glared furiously at them, pawed the earth, bellowed loudly, and rattled the boards by banging its horns against them.

"I'm glad he's not loose," Chet said fervently.

"So am I," Joe agreed.

The boys walked through the gate into the pasture. The big maple on the other side gave them their bearings, and they walked toward it at a rapid pace. Beyond it, the broad expanse of fields and meadows was broken only by an occasional tree or shrub.

Chet brought up the subject of Crow Morven. "We're not his favorite people," he observed. "Maybe he gave us a bum steer about walking to Juniper Field. You think we should go back and take the car?"

"No way." Frank grinned at the hopeful tone in Chet's voice. "We go by leg-mobile."

"Morven has no reason to give us a bum steer," Joe affirmed. "We'd find out how to get there anyway, and we'd know he was lying. He wouldn't want that to happen. Not if he's up to something."

"I sure wish somebody would come along and give us a lift." Chet sighed.

They were about in the middle of the pasture when suddenly the earth seemed to shake behind them. They heard the pounding of hooves in their direction.

Whirling around, they were appalled to see that the bull was out of its pen and dashing toward them. Its eyes were fiery with rage, and steam spouted from its nostrils. It shook its horns savagely as it hurtled forward at terrific speed!

Chet had moved a little to one side during the walk. The bull singled him out and headed straight toward him. Chet turned to run but stumbled and fell. The bull, lowering its horns, lunged forward to gore him!

8

Disguise and Alias?

In a flash, Frank took off his rust-colored shirt and draped it to one side like a bullfighter's cape. He caught the attention of the enraged beast, and it charged the shirt, stomping past Chet, missing him by a hairsbreadth. Frank moved the shirt farther away from his friend, and again the bull went for it in a violent attack.

As the Hardy boy maneuvered the bull into following the shirt, Chet scrambled to his feet. He ran to a nearby tree, climbed into it, and peered frantically through the branches.

Frank continued to play the role of matador with a cape. Stepping backward, he shifted the shirt from one position to another, each time goading the bull into another charge. Slowly but surely the boy guided the animal back to its pen. Its final charge sent it careening through the gate. Joe, who had followed his brother, locked the bull in with a shout of relief.

"You should have been a bullfighter, Frank," he said.

"No thanks. I don't want to be anywhere around if that brute escapes again."

Joe tried to secure the lock of the pen but found that the latch refused to stay in place. "The screw's loose!" he exclaimed. "Won't hold the gate closed properly. Somebody did it deliberately. I wonder if Crow Morven's responsible for the bull getting out?"

"He might have set us up when he told us to go through the pasture," Frank said. "Then he unscrewed the latch after he left the house. But we have no proof."

Joe took a small, multipurpose screwdriver out of his pocket and tightened the screw on the latch, while Frank examined his shirt. Finding nothing worse than a tear at the bottom where the bull had gored it, he put the shirt back on and they rejoined Chet, who was still up in the tree.

"Is it safe to come down?" he asked apprehensively.

"Sure it is," Frank said, and the three resumed their walk across the pasture. Near the tall maple they found a gate, went through, and saw the path leading into the woods. Recognizing the two boulders Morven had mentioned, they continued on. A small plane zoomed low overhead and vanished beyond the treetops. They heard the sound of motors revving up, and when they reached the end of the woods, they were on the outskirts of the airport.

The plane they had seen was taxiing to a stop in front of the control tower. Another one was swinging around for a thrust down the runway into takeoff. A number of small craft were parked around the perimeter of the airfield.

A single helicopter stood behind the control tower. It bore the painted legend JF333 on its side.

"That's our chopper," Joe said. "The one we saw grab the *Flashing Arrow!*"

"Let's check it out," Chet suggested, walking toward the helicopter.

Frank restrained him. "Not yet. We'll have to get an okay at the office first. Otherwise it might be the lockup for us if the owner blows the whistle."

At the office, Frank asked the clerk who owned the helicopter.

"We do," was the answer. "Juniper Field. The chopper's for hire."

"Was it rented recently?"

"Just last night. Why the questions?"

To avert suspicion, Frank said, "We might want

to take it out. Mind if we have a look?"

"Be my guest," the clerk offered.

"Can you tell us who hired the helicopter last night?" Joe queried casually.

"A tall man wearing a black beard and dark glasses." The clerk consulted his register. "His name is John Jones according to his flying license. He landed back here, paid his fee, and left."

When the boys were outside the office again, Frank remarked, "Sounds like a disguise, and the name has to be an alias, too!"

"Well, he couldn't have been Crow Morven," Chet pointed out. "Morven was on the ground when the chopper came over."

The helicopter was a small model with a single set of rotary blades. The cockpit, protected by wraparound unbreakable glass that allowed a view from side to side as well as in front, had seats at the instrument panel for pilot and copilot. A compartment in the rear permitted a passenger to be squeezed in.

The rear compartment also held the winch, a spinning drum worked by hydraulic controls. The tail of the helicopter formed a mesh of metal struts, designed to give balance in the air. The landing gear terminate in three wheels, two up ahead and one behind.

The craft showed signs of use the previous night. There were oil stains on the fuselage beneath the blades and the wheels were caked with mud.

"There must have been two guys last night," Frank observed. "The pilot and a man to work the winch."

Chet climbed into the back seat and began to spin the winch. "No cable or grappling iron in here," he informed Frank and Joe, who had gotten into the front. "They must have taken them away."

"Along with the *Flashing Arrow*," Joe said morosely.

The Hardys, who were experienced pilots, examined the instrument panel. "I wish we could go for a spin," Frank said. "I'll bet this whirlybird works like a charm."

"We saw that last night," Joe reminded him. "The pilot could have landed in our laps if he'd wanted to. I hope he left his calling card in here."

They spent half an hour searching the craft for a clue, but all they found were pamphlets on such things as flying rules, airport regulations, and maintenance instructions for the helicopter.

"No luck," Frank said disgustedly. "Let's get out of here." As he turned, he brushed against the front seats, sweeping a folded piece of paper onto the floor of the cockpit. A flash of red caught Joe's eye. He picked up the paper and was astounded to see a hex sign!

Someone had drawn in colored ink the red pentagram in a white square inside a black circle. The three boys looked in fascination at the mystic symbol.

"That's Mr. Hammerley's hex!" Chet burst out.

"Is there anything on the other side?" Frank asked.

Joe turned the paper over. It said in large printed letters: CHESAPEAKE CROSSING. Apart from that, the paper was blank.

Chet scratched his head. "I never heard of Chesapeake Crossing. Is it a town?"

"Yes, on Chesapeake Bay," Joe replied.

The boys descended from the helicopter, and, returning to the office, they told the clerk they were not going to hire the helicopter after all. Then they headed for the police station of the nearby town to ask about the stolen weather vanes.

The sergeant on duty said, "We haven't had a break in the case yet."

"Are there no clues at all?" Frank asked.

"The only thing we heard from an informer is that there's a fence for stolen weather vanes in the Chesapeake area of Maryland."

The boys stared in amazement but did not reveal their clue.

"Our informer doesn't know where the fence is," the sergeant went on, "but the Maryland police are checking on it. That's all I can tell you."

Outside headquarters, Joe commented, "Looks

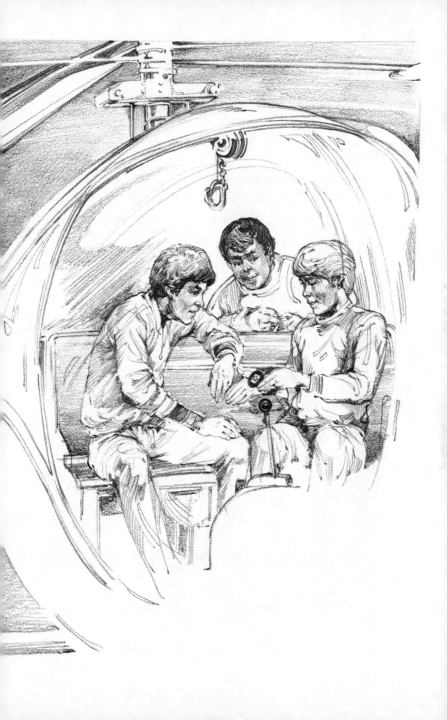

as if we'd better go to Chesapeake Crossing. That may be where the *Flashing Arrow* is, along with all the other weather vanes that disappeared around here."

Frank nodded. "Besides, Dad's in Washington. We'll still be near enough to give him a hand if he needs us on his spy case."

Strolling through the town, the boys came to the county historical museum. It was a single-story building with wings on either side.

A sign on the front door proclaimed:

WEATHER VANE EXHIBITION

"Let's go in," Frank proposed. "It might give us an idea."

They were the only visitors. The curator came out of his office. He was a plump, jolly man in white ducks, white shirt, and horn-rimmed glasses, who introduced himself as Gaspard Clay. He had a habit of clearing his throat as he spoke.

"Since you are the only ones here today, ahem, let me show you around," he offered. "You can see the whole museum, except, ahem, for the west wing, which is closed to the public because it's undergoing repairs."

"We'd like to see the weather vane exhibit," Joe informed him.

"Right this way. It's in the, ahem, east wing."

About a hundred weather vanes lined the walls of a large room or stood mounted on a long table. There were all sizes and shapes, some of wood, others of metal. Many portrayed animals, others formed stars, crescent moons, or sunbursts.

Clay bustled around discoursing volubly on the importance of weather vanes. "In the days before radio and television, ahem, farmers depended on them to tell which way the wind was blowing. Then they could judge whether rain was coming. Of course," he added with a smile, "weather vanes could not make long-range forecasts. But they were useful in foretelling the day's weather."

Before the boys left the exhibit, Joe mentioned their robbery case. "Mr. Clay, do you know anything about the stolen weather vanes?"

"Of course I know. I keep track of every weather vane in the county. Some of the pieces I remember best are gone."

"But you have no idea who took them?"

"None. I suppose you have heard about, ahem, the *Galloping Rider?* It's terrible to think of it being stolen."

"Yes," Frank agreed. "We're investigating that theft and the others."

"We saw the *Galloping Rider* at an auction!" Chet piped up and told about the incident.

"Well, I hope you have better luck the next time,"

said Gaspard Clay. "The man who took it ought to be in jail. If anyone tries to palm the *Galloping Rider* off on the museum, ahem, I'll let you know."

"You can reach us at the Hammerley farm," Joe said.

"Ah yes, the barn with the *Flashing Arrow*. It's a beautiful and very valuable antique."

"It was heisted last night!" Chet blurted.

Clay shook his head in dismay. "That's too bad. It was the masterpiece of all weather vanes in the county."

"Does Chesapeake Crossing mean anything to you?" Joe spoke up.

The curator smiled. "It sure does!" he boomed.

9

The Suspect

Startled, the boys stared at him. They wondered if this was the breakthrough they were waiting for.

"It means the very best crabbing there is," Clay went on jovially. "I go down to Chesapeake Crossing whenever I can. From there, you have two hundred miles of bay loaded with crab."

Again the Hardys felt disappointed. Only Chet was pleased by the curator's remarks. The word *crab* gave him delicious visions of steamed crustaceans served for dinner.

"There's a marina at Chesapeake Crossing," Clay continued. "You can rent a boat and head for the coves and inlets where the crabs are. All you need is a net, ahem, to make a big catch. I usually steam some of them on the shore and bring the rest home. I have a wonderful recipe for crab if you'd like to hear it."

Chet's eyes lit up, but Frank said hastily, "Not now, Mr. Clay. We have to get back to the Hammerley farm."

Clay shook hands with the boys in a friendly fashion. "If there's anything I can do to help you solve the weather vane mystery, please let me know," he offered.

The young detectives promised to do so, then left the museum and returned to Juniper Field. From there they began the long trek back to the farm. Chet was puffing when they arrived. His face was red and his feet felt sore.

Mrs. Smith told the boys that the farmer was out in the pasture. She added that he had phoned the police about the stolen weather vane and the drugged cocoa. Two officers in a patrol car had arrived and searched the farm but left without finding any clue.

Noting that the boys were hot and tired, the housekeeper brought them a pitcher of lemonade and a plate of cookies. Gratefully the trio dug into the refreshments, when the phone rang. It was Fenton Hardy.

"What have you been doing since we talked?" Mr. Hardy asked. "Any developments in the weather vane case?"

Frank described the theft of the *Flashing Arrow* while the boys had been guarding the loft.

"Those crooks are clever," Mr. Hardy noted. "Have you been able to trace the helicopter?"

Joe explained the discovery of the chopper at Juniper Field and the paper bearing the Hammerley hex sign along with the reference to Chesapeake Crossing.

"Chesapeake Crossing!" Mr. Hardy exclaimed. "Why, that's the place where Clifford Hunter was last seen!"

"His sailboat has not been found?" Frank asked.

"No. The navy has been watching not only Chesapeake Crossing, but the entire eastern coast very closely ever since he vanished, but he has not been sighted."

"I take it the owner of the marina where he kept his boat has been questioned?" Frank suggested.

"Yes. But he could shed no light on the matter. At first nobody thought anything about Hunter's failing to return, because every now and then he made runs down Chesapeake Bay that lasted for a few days. Besides, they knew the weather was good, so there was no reason to fear he sank in a storm."

"Maybe Hunter got stranded on an island in the bay," Joe said.

"Unlikely," Mr. Hardy replied. "Hunter's an expert sailor who knows every mile of the bay. Still, the navy sent out scouting planes to look for him. They didn't find a thing. I'm on my way to Chesapeake Crossing now to investigate."

"We're on our way there, too," Frank revealed. "Let's meet and compare notes."

Their father chuckled. "Not so fast. You've got another assignment first. I want you to go to Washington. I've arranged a briefing for you at the Pentagon. Be sure you've got your I.D. cards with you."

"What do we do when we get there?" Joe questioned.

"Ask for Joseph Wickerson. He's the head of the navy department where Clifford Hunter worked. He'll give you the details about the missing document. After the briefing, go on to Chesapeake Crossing. We'll meet and see if we can crack the spy case. Maybe we'll get lucky and solve the weather vane mystery at the same time. I'll be at the Sunset Motel."

After a little more conversation, Fenton Hardy hung up. Frank and Joe started back to rejoin Chet. Through the kitchen door they spotted Mrs. Smith standing at the sink. She was holding a cocoa can in her hand.

Frank nudged Joe. "I heard Mr. Hammerley say he's keeping the cocoa locked in the pantry so no one can spike it with knockout drops," he said in an undertone.

"Mrs. Smith must have a key to the pantry he doesn't know about," Joe whispered. "Let's watch her."

Mrs. Smith turned away from the sink and walked out of the kitchen. The Hardys followed her upstairs, where she went into one of the bedrooms.

"That must be Mr. Hammerley's room," Frank murmured. "She's making his cocoa for tonight. Maybe with knockout drops in it!"

"That means Mrs. Smith is a member of the gang and that they're planning something else!"

Frank nodded soberly. Together they tiptoed up to the door and cautiously peered into the bedroom. Mrs. Smith was standing at a bedside table with her back to them. She still held the cocoa can in her hand. Breathlessly they waited for her next move, hoping to catch her red-handed in the act of spiking Hammerley's nighttime drink.

As they watched, the housekeeper leaned toward a shelf on the wall near the bed and poured water from the cocoa can into the pot of a large philodendron.

Ruefully the Hardys grinned at one another. They were about to retreat silently when Mrs. Smith turned around and saw them.

"I want to talk to you boys," she declared.

"Uh-oh," Frank thought. "Here's where we get it for spying on her."

"It's about last night," Mrs. Smith continued.

"What about it?" Joe asked.

"Well, when I brought Mr. Hammerley's cocoa here to the bedroom, I heard footsteps downstairs. They surprised me because Mr. Hammerley was in bed and the rest of the workers were gone for the night. I thought I must be hearing things, except for what I saw when I got back to the kitchen."

"What was that, Mrs. Smith?" Frank inquired eagerly.

"One of the kitchen windows was unlocked. I always lock all of them before I serve the cocoa and leave. Someone was in the kitchen while I was upstairs! I didn't think of it this morning, with all the excitement, but now I remember."

"What did you do then?" Joe asked.

"I locked the window again, checked that the house was empty, and went home."

"Well, whoever unlocked the window couldn't have drugged the cocoa, because you were already serving it," Frank pointed out.

Joe snapped his fingers. "I've got it! The person who drugged the cocoa sneaked back and un-locked the window so he could get in during the night and destroy the evidence. You sure foxed him, Mrs. Smith. He must have been ready to blow his top when he came back later and tried to get in! You saved vital evidence without knowing it!"

The housekeeper seemed pleased as she accompanied the Hardys downstairs, excited that she was taking part in one of their cases.

When Mr. Hammerley came in, he listened to their plan to go to Chesapeake Crossing. "I don't know anything about the place," he admitted. "But I don't mind where you go, as long as you get the *Flashing Arrow* back. When are you leaving?"

"Tomorrow morning," Frank replied, without adding that the boys would stop in Washington before proceeding to their destination. The young detective did not want to upset Hammerley by revealing that they were working on the spy case as well as his weather vane mystery.

"Is there anything else you'd like to know about before you go?" Hammerley inquired.

"Do you suspect anybody here at the farm as a possible accomplice of the thieves?" Frank asked.

"I don't suspect anyone working for me at the moment," Hammerley replied. "But I fired a man two weeks ago because he was loitering around the house and I caught him stealing food. I never thought he might steal my weather vane, though. His name is Ed Bryle."

"Where can we find him?" Joe wanted to know.

"I have no idea. I paid him and he left without telling me where he was going."

"Do you happen to have a photograph of him?" Frank inquired.

Hammerley nodded. He went to a desk and

withdrew a picture from a drawer, then handed it to Frank, who examined it while Joe and Chet were looking over his shoulder. Bryle was a short, wizened man dressed in farm overalls.

"That's the man we saw at the auction!" Frank gasped. "The one who grabbed the *Galloping Rider* from Joe and ran off with it!"

Just then the telephone rang. Mrs. Smith said it was another call for the Hardys.

"Must be Dad again," Frank guessed and took the receiver while Joe stood close enough to listen in.

A weird, squeaky voice warned, "Hardys, beware of the hex!"

10

Danger in the Driveway

The phone clicked off. Frank held it in his hand for a moment, puzzled. Then he hung up and turned to Joe. "Did you recognize the voice?"

Joe shook his head. "Sounded like a real weirdo. I never heard anything like it."

"Neither have I. But it seems as if the weather vane gang will stop at nothing to get rid of us!"

"Which means we'd better keep our eyes open from here on out. They might send a hit man to take us off the case—permanently."

When the boys reported the warning to Chet and Hammerley, the two were perplexed.

"I don't know anyone with the kind of voice you describe," Hammerley said. "Could it be a hoax?"

Frank shrugged. "We'll have to solve the case before we can answer that."

Next morning, Chet received a phone call from Iola. She informed him that he had been chosen to represent Bayport High in a state archery competition. Knowing how badly he wanted to compete, Frank and Joe persuaded their friend to participate.

"We'll be meeting Dad," Joe pointed out. "He'll back us up."

"Just win the honors for good old Bayport," Frank added. "You can come to Washington with us and then catch a plane home."

After breakfast, the boys went outside to their rented car, which a farmhand had brought around the driveway and parked in front of the house. They were standing beside the car talking to Hammerley, when Crow Morven drove a pickup truck to the top of an incline leading into the driveway. The foreman jumped out of the vehicle and approached the group.

Suddenly the pickup began to move. Gathering speed, it hurtled down the slope directly toward the boys!

Frank saw it and barely had time to shout a warning. Chet and Hammerley dived into the bushes bordering the driveway, while Joe, who stood closest to the pickup's path, leaped onto the vehicle and wrenched the door open. He slid behind the wheel and managed to put on the brakes.

Morven had run behind the truck and was shouting excitedly. When he reached the group, Frank glared at him. "You aimed that pickup at us!"

"I forgot to put the brake on. It wasn't intentional, believe me!" the foreman insisted. But he grinned evilly as he spoke.

Chet waved a fist under his nose. "Next time, it'll be intentional. And I mean a collision of your nose and my fist!"

Hammerley watched the heated exchange with a worried frown. "Crow, I'm sure you didn't mean to hurt anybody, but you must be more careful in the future."

"Sure, Mr. Hammerley," Morven replied and walked away.

Joe parked the vehicle, then returned to his friends. They got into their car, said good-bye to the farmer, and drove off with Joe behind the wheel. About three miles down the road they saw a horse and carriage racing toward them. Afraid of an accident, Joe pulled to the right and stopped, letting the engine idle. The horse came to a halt in a cloud of dust as the driver tugged hard on its reins. It was the same wild-eyed woman with unkempt hair blowing in the wind, who had spoken to them previously!

"It's Mad Maggie!" Frank exclaimed.

"*Ja*, Mad Maggie!" she shouted. "And my friend is with me, see?"

She lifted a birdcage from the seat beside her and held it up. A large horned owl stared at the boys from between the bars.

"Is that a witch's owl?" Joe wanted to know.

"*Ja*, it is."

"Does it talk?"

"*Ja*, it talks. Listen." Leaning over the cage, she urged the owl. "All right, my pretty one. What do you say to these boys from Bayport who have come to the Pennsylvania Dutch country?"

The owl fluttered its wings and hooted.

Chet felt an eerie sensation, as if a clammy hand gripped his shoulder. He gulped as the sound grated on his ears. "Wh-what did your friend say?" he asked.

"It said the hex is working. Ye should have gone home when Mad Maggie warned ye."

Chet glanced at Joe. "I wish he'd start the car and get us out of here before she rides off on a broomstick!" he thought to himself.

The owl gave another low hoot that choked off suddenly.

"Do ye know what that means?" Mad Maggie demanded. "It means—when the weather is stormy, your search is in vain!"

94

Joe was dumbfounded. Could the words *weather* and *vain* be a code referring to the weather vane mystery?

"The rider gallops, the arrow flashes!" Mad Maggie went on.

Frank stared at her. "Are you talking about the *Galloping Rider* and the *Flashing Arrow*?" he inquired.

"*Ja*, that I do. They have flown away from here. My owl says so."

"Where have they flown to? Can your owl tell us?"

Maggie leaned over and whispered something in the owl's ear, all the while keeping her eyes fixed on the boys. This time the bird made no sound. It closed its eyes and appeared to be asleep.

"The place is secret!" Mad Maggie hissed. With that, she pulled the reins of her horse and drove off.

Joe headed in the opposite direction. "You think she really knows something?" he asked.

Frank shrugged. "Apparently she's heard of the thefts. But so has everybody in the county."

"She could be the squeaky voice you heard over the phone," Chet suggested.

"It's possible," Frank conceded. "The crooks might have hired her to scare us away."

"She succeeded, as far as I'm concerned," Chet declared. "I'm glad we're getting out of here!"

They came to the place where they had seen the auction. A couple of men were folding the tent and stacking the pegs. A third was loading unsold objects into a truck.

Joshua Korbo was showing his auctioneer's license to a county official who towered a good three inches over him.

"How was business?" Joe greeted Korbo after pulling up alongside the two men.

The auctioneer pushed his steel-rimmed glasses from his nose up onto his forehead. "Very good," he snapped, "in spite of what your fat friend did to my tent!"

Insulted, Chet was about to snap back when Frank spoke up. "Have you found any sign of the weather vane, the *Galloping Rider?*"

"None. I doubt it was ever here."

"We saw it!" Chet insisted.

"That's what *you* say." Korbo shrugged, then turned to talk to one of his assistants.

"I get the feeling he doesn't want to tell us anything," Joe said and drove on.

Frank chuckled. "He's still mad at Chet for knocking over his tent."

They continued in silence for a while. Then a big black car zoomed past them. The driver was a man in a black beard and dark glasses. He fitted the description of the individual who had hired the helicopter that snatched the *Flashing Arrow!*

"This could be our suspect!" Frank cried out. "Don't lose him, Joe!"

His brother trod hard on the accelerator, and the speedometer rose to the legal limit as they sped after him. Seeing he was being followed, the black-bearded man suddenly turned onto a side road. Joe reacted just in time to make the turn himself. He had to grip the steering wheel firmly to keep it from being torn from his grasp as he jounced over rocks and potholes.

The wild pursuit led far out into the country, where the man ahead tried to shake the boys by driving down country lanes and across open fields. He kept glancing over his shoulder to see how close they were. At one point they got near enough to see sunlight glinting off his dark glasses.

"He's our man all right," Chet said. "If he had nothing to hide, why would he try to get away from us?"

Joe stuck grimly to the trail, narrowing the gap whenever he could. But another turn by the fugitive made him lose ground on a cow path. Then he had to slow down because an Amish farmer in a buggy came between the two cars. The boys saw the black beard shoot along a bumpy dirt road into the woods and disappear among the trees. Joe followed as fast as he could, whipping past country lanes and down more cow paths.

"I hope this is the right road," he grated. "If you see that big black car, tell me."

"Will do," Frank said, shading his eyes with his hand and gazing into the distance.

"I wish that guy would stick to the freeway," Chet protested. Their rotund companion was sore from being bounced up and down in the back seat.

A moment later they rounded a curve at top speed. A large black car stood in the middle of the road, blocking their passage, and they were hurtling toward it!

Twisting the steering wheel violently to one side, Joe narrowly avoided a collision. His car flipped up on two wheels, as if it were going to turn over, righted itself at the last moment, and halted joltingly in a ditch.

The next moment the door on Joe's side was wrenched open and a harsh voice snarled, "Okay, you punks! The chase is over. This is the end of the road for you!"

11

Boys in Trouble

"Get out!" the voice commanded. "Resistance will get you nowhere!"

Frank, Joe, and Chet emerged from the car and found themselves confronted by two state police officers.

"Is this your car?" the older one demanded in a stern tone.

"No, it isn't," Joe replied.

"So you stole it!" the officer accused them. "We had a tip you guys were operating in this area. Figured you'd be coming down this road and set up our block in just the right place."

"Where have you stashed the other stolen cars?" the policeman demanded. "Of course you don't have to answer. You have a right to remain silent."

"That won't be necessary," Frank said evenly. "You've got it all wrong."

"No, we've got it dead right! You're the gang that's been stealing cars all over the county. We're taking you in. The charge is grand larceny."

Interrupted by the radio in the unmarked patrol car, the policeman walked over and answered the call, while his partner kept the boys covered. When the officer returned to the group, he shook his head.

"The stolen-car gang was arrested a few minutes ago up the road," he revealed.

"Then who are these guys?" his partner wanted to know.

The boys quickly identified themselves, and the officers were impressed to learn that Frank and Joe were the sons of Fenton Hardy, who was known to lawmen throughout the nation.

"We're sorry about mistaking you for the thieves," the older officer said. "But you did come down the road lickety-split, as if you were trying to get away as fast as possible."

"Actually, we were following a suspect," Frank said. "That's why we were going at such speed."

"Are you on a case?"

Frank mentioned the stolen weather vane mystery and inquired if the officers had seen a tall man in a black beard and dark glasses driving a big black car. But the policemen had not seen the suspect.

"He must have turned off this road onto a side lane before he reached our roadblock," the younger one said. "He could be in the next county by now." He promised to let the Hardys know if they encountered the suspect, then the three boys continued their drive to Washington. They managed to pick up Route 222, which took them past Pennsylvania's Brandywine Battlefield Park and across the Susquehanna River to Route 95. When they crossed an arm of Chesapeake Bay near Baltimore, they were set on a direct course toward the Potomac River.

After driving through Maryland and down the long Baltimore-Washington Parkway, they reached their destination.

"I could use some chow," Chet suggested.

"So could I," Frank admitted.

"That makes it unanimous," Joe said with a grin and wheeled into the parking lot of a diner.

The boys went inside and sat at a table by the window, where they could watch the flow of traffic outside. After a quick meal, Frank decided to call Joseph Wickerson's office. A secretary informed him that Wickerson could see them in about two hours. Then Chet telephoned the airport and made reservations on a flight from Washington to Bayport later in the afternoon.

The three agreed to kill time by doing some sight-seeing on their way to the Pentagon. They paid the cashier and were walking toward the exit with Chet in the lead, when a glint of dark glasses reflected momentarily in the plate-glass window and then vanished.

"That's the guy we're after!" Chet exclaimed. "I'm sure of it! Come on!" He wedged himself through the revolving door, helped by pressure from Frank and Joe who were behind him. They caught a fleeting glimpse of a figure turning the corner of the diner, then a car door slammed shut in the parking area.

"I'll stop him!" Chet declared and hurried to the strip of drive leading to the street. He raised his hand as a large black car approached. The Hardys ran up to him. They had not seen the person Chet was after but assumed that he knew what he was doing.

The black car stopped in front of Chet and the driver rolled down the window. She was a pretty brunette, who now pushed her sunglasses up on her head. "Why are you stopping me?" she asked curiously.

Chet turned beet red. "I'm sorry," he stammered. "I mistook you for someone else."

He stepped aside and let the car pass. "Don't kid me," he begged the Hardys.

Frank suppressed a smile. "We won't kid you, Chet. A detective has to move fast sometimes, and mistakes do happen."

Chet recovered from his embarrassment and they returned to their car. Soon they were driving up Capitol Hill to the juncture of Pennslyvania Avenue and Independence Avenue. They passed the Library of Congress and swung around the Capitol building.

"That's where Congress holds its meetings," Chet pointed out. "I'll bet they're helping the Hardys in there right now."

"They are?" Frank raised his eyebrows.

"Crime laws!" Chet explained. "Making it easier for you to nab the bad guys."

"Thanks a lot for the compliment, Chet." Frank laughed. "But I think Congress is more interested in helping the FBI than in helping us."

"Well, there's the FBI," Joe said and pointed toward the Justice Department. "Boy, what a crime lab they have!"

The Hardys had visited the FBI lab while working for their father. They had checked fingerprints in the FBI files, tested firearms in the ballistics department, and consulted the bureau's cryptographers on the best methods of breaking codes.

"Too bad we don't have time to drop in and say

hello," Frank commented. "Maybe we will on our next trip to Washington."

"I'd like to drop in on the president," Chet declared. "I'd tell him a thing or two on how to run the country."

"Like bows and arrows for the infantry," Joe joked. "Well, we'd better be getting to the Pentagon." He swerved onto Seventeenth Street, swung around the Washington Monument, and drove down Fifteenth Street past the Tidal Basin and the Jefferson Memorial across the Potomac to the south parking area of the Pentagon.

He pulled into a public parking lot, and the boys could see the famous military building beyond hundreds of parked cars lined up in double rows. An open space with grass, trees, and driving lanes led up to the broad facade of the Pentagon on their side. They got out and the Hardys escorted Chet to a bus stop.

Their friend was downcast. "I wish I could go with you," he lamented. "I'd like to stay on the case."

"You're still on the case," Joe reassured him. "You're just taking time out to shoot some arrows in Bayport."

"And if we haven't solved the mystery by the time the archery contest is over, we'll send you an SOS," Frank added.

Chet cheered up as he climbed into the bus. He grinned at them from the window, then the vehicle pulled away to go to the airport.

Frank and Joe gazed up at the enormous five-sided building from which the secretary of defense and the Joint Chiefs of Staff ran the United States Armed Forces.

"Come on, Joe. Let's go in," Frank said.

Joe chuckled. "Maybe if we stay long enough, we'll come out three-star generals!"

12

Pentagon Briefing

From South Parking, the Hardys entered the Pentagon through the river entrance and asked for Joseph Wickerson at the information desk. The receptionist put through a call and handed the phone to Frank.

"Wickerson here," Frank heard. "I'm finishing a report for the chief of naval operations. Come up in forty-five minutes. The room is 5E600. See you then." Wickerson hung up.

Frank asked the receptionist how to get to room 5E600.

"It's on the fifth floor of ring E," she explained. "The Pentagon has five floors, and there are five rings on each floor, lettered outward from the center from A to E. For instance, 1A means the first ring of the first floor, 2B means the second ring of the second floor, and so on. So, 5E means the fifth ring of the fifth floor. When you get there, look for room 600."

With time to kill before their appointment, the Hardys strolled around the Pentagon. Joe bought a guidebook to the building at a newsstand and flipped through it.

"Each of the five sides of the Pentagon is over nine hundred feet long. That's three times the length of a football field," he told Frank.

"I'd rather carry the ball on Bayport High field," Frank responded. "You'd need a lot more blockers here to score a touchdown."

He was referring to the crowds moving through the building. Civilian employees hurried in all directions. Men and women in military uniforms were reporting for their daily assignments. The Hardys noticed high-ranking officers of the army, navy, and air force walking by rapidly and saying little.

"The big brass seem bothered by something," Joe observed.

"I'll bet they're worried about Clifford Hunter and the missing document," Frank replied. "From what Dad said, if the submarine plan is gone for good, our whole military establishment is in big trouble."

The Hardys went up to the second floor, noticing that only the stairs and escalators were available to them. The elevators were restricted to freight and other heavy cargo.

They walked along corridors decorated with pictures of military history from the Trojan War to the Thor Missile. When they passed the office of the Joint Chiefs of Staff, they saw a sign warning, "Admittance by Authorized Credentials Only."

Frank remarked, "Our I.D. cards won't get us in there. We'd be stopped by the guard." Then he looked at his wristwatch. "Our forty-five minutes are nearly up. Let's go upstairs."

Continuing to the top floor, the boys reached ring 5E. They showed their identification and were allowed to pass. When they found room 600, Frank knocked, and a moment later the door swung open.

Joseph Wickerson, a burly man with a genial smile, welcomed them into his office. A desk stood at the window, with two chairs facing it, and there was a sofa in one corner. Maps of American naval installations and pictures of naval warfare lined the walls. One picture showed the first nuclear submarine, the *Nautilus*, about to dive.

Motioning the boys into the two chairs, Wickerson sat behind his desk. He clasped his hands and looked at them with a serious expression.

"How much has your father told you about the navy's spy mystery?" he asked.

"We know a classified document belonging to the navy is missing," Joe replied.

"Also, a civilian employee has disappeared," Frank added. "A man named Clifford Hunter."

Wickerson thumped his fist on the desk. "We've got to find Cliff Hunter. That's why we want you two on the case with your father. I'll explain the spy problem in a moment. But first I'd better give you the facts about the missing document."

Wickerson pushed a button and ordered, "Tell Archie Olson to bring the MASUB plan."

While they were waiting, Wickerson gave the boys a brief explanation of MASUB. "It stands for maser submarine. My department is perfecting a new device that uses maser beams for deep-water navigation. Cliff Hunter had responsibility for the scientific research, and Archie Olson drew up the blueprints. Both worked under my supervision. Do you know the meaning of *maser?*"

Frank replied, "Microwave amplification by stimulated emission of radiation. We've been studying masers in our high-school physics lab."

"Masers are stronger radio waves," Joe recalled. "You trap atomic energy in crystals and increase the energy by hitting the crystals with atomic particles. A wave shoots out that's longer and stronger than a radio wave."

"You've stated the science in a nutshell," Wickerson complimented them. "Well, the U.S. Navy has added a wrinkle that nobody else knows about. I hope!" he added in an obvious reference to Hunter's disappearance.

"Who made the breakthrough?" Frank inquired.

"Cliff Hunter!" Wickerson boomed. "That's why we have to find him quickly. He has not only the document but also a lot of advanced nautical science in his head. A foreign power could use his knowledge of laboratory research to endanger the U.S.A."

A knock on the door brought Archie Olson on the scene. A tall, thin man with a faraway look in his eyes, he spread the blueprint of MASUB on the desk. Taking a slide rule from his pocket, he pointed to its most important features.

"The key to our breakthrough," he revealed, "is that we can link masers end on end indefinitely— around the world if we want to. It's done by a computer that tells the atomic propulsion device of a nuclear sub when to release the next maser and in what direction. The captain and crew can go to sleep for the voyage. The masers will take them to their destination automatically."

Olson showed sketches of maser-producing crystals and demonstrated the relationship between the computer and the crystals. Then he explained how a computer could be programmed to keep the masers lined up.

"Can't the masers be detected?" Joe asked.

Olson shook his head. "They're protected by a nuclear shield. Here's the blueprint for the shield. Cliff Hunter worked out the formula."

Olson paused and looked at Wickerson, clearly wondering whether he should have mentioned Hunter.

"It's all right," Wickerson advised him. "Frank and Joe know about Hunter. In fact, they're in on the search for him."

After more discussion of maser and nuclear subs, Olson left, taking the blueprint with him.

Wickerson said thoughtfully, "The missing document is the original blueprint of the maser-producing crystals and their linkage to the computer. It's marked **MASUB TOP-SECRET.** When you see those words, you'll know you've found the plan Hunter took."

"Did you suspect he was a spy?" Frank queried.

Wickerson shrugged. "No, otherwise I'd have turned him in to the Pentagon security forces. But I thought there was something fishy about him after the Cosmo Rocket episode."

"What was that?"

"The navy has a classified project on a revolutionary new type of missile for our surface fleet. It's being developed by another department, and the members of my department have to get special

111

clearance to look at the Cosmo Rocket files. Two weeks ago I needed to examine those files, so I got clearance and went in.

"I was surprised to see Hunter at the files. I asked what he was doing there, and he said he had clearance for some work concerning the connection between the navigational systems of subs and rockets.

"Since he was one of my trusted assistants, I didn't pursue the matter—unfortunately, because I know now that his clearance was forged!"

"Did he do anything else to make you suspect him?" Joe inquired.

"Well, he seemed to be always sneaking around and poking into things that weren't his business. Looking through the papers of other scientists, things like that. But I must confess it didn't occur to me that he might be a spy."

"Do you think he stole anything else?"

Wickerson tapped his fingers on the desk. "As far as I know, nothing else is gone. I run a tight ship, and only the MASUB document is missing from my files. I daresay Hunter fled because he knew he couldn't play the same trick on me twice.

"Of course, he got away with an immensely valuable blueprint. So, perhaps he figured one theft was enough. He'll be wealthy if he sells it to a foreign power."

The Hardys inquired about the discovery that the MASUB document was missing.

Wickerson frowned. "I summoned Hunter into this office the day before the discovery to discuss some bugs in MASUB. We went over the problems and ironed them out. At the end, I put the blueprint in this desk drawer, and we agreed to carry on the discussion the following day. We left the office and I locked the door and went home.

"When I got here in the morning, the blueprint was gone. I called the lab to have Hunter report to me at once. He wasn't there. So I asked them to send Archie Olson, who told me he saw Hunter leaving my office after hours the night before. Archie thought I was in the office at the time. Actually, I was out of the building."

"Hunter must have had a key to the office, since he came back after you left," Joe inferred.

Wickerson nodded. "He wasn't supposed to, but I imagine he contrived in some underhanded way to have a duplicate made. I wouldn't put it past him. He's a clever fellow. That's why he's so dangerous."

"What did he do after leaving your office?" Joe wondered.

Wickerson slammed the table in disgust. "He simply walked out of the building as he did every evening. Only this time he was carrying the MASUB document with him. At first it didn't hit me that anything was really wrong. I thought he'd come in with a good explanation. When I couldn't find him anywhere, I realized he had fled. Then came word that he was last seen at Chelski's Marina in Chesapeake Crossing. And now you know as much as I do."

"We're going from here to Chesapeake Crossing," Frank said. "We'll try to pick up his trail from there."

"Well, I'm glad I have you boys on the case," Wickerson assured them. "After all, you're sons of Fenton Hardy, who has done vital undercover work for the Pentagon in the past. You'll do your country a great service if you find Hunter and retrieve the sub blueprint he took."

Promising they would do their best, the Hardys left Wickerson's office and descended to the concourse of the Pentagon. They passed an exhibition of navy exploration in the waters around the Antarctic continent.

Joe paused for a look. "Frank, they've got a lot of mysteries to solve down there," he said with a smile.

"Yes, but no one can waltz off with the evidence. It would be a long swim home."

They went to South Parking, where Frank started the car and headed for an exit. He was nearly there when a car flashed out of a parking slot and cut in front of him. Frank hit the brakes in an effort to prevent a collision!

114

13

Surprise Encounter

The car stopped with a jolt that threw Joe heavily against the dashboard. The speeding car flew out the exit and roared off toward the Potomac.

Frank stared after it. "Joe, did you see who that driver was?"

Joe flopped back in his seat and rubbed his twisted shoulder. "No. Did you?"

"I sure did. He was Archie Olson!"

Joe winced in pain. "Olson may be a whiz of a scientist, but he's a lousy driver! He nearly racked us up!"

"Maybe he did it deliberately."

Joe stared at his brother. "But why would he do a thing like that? If you hadn't hit the brakes so fast, he'd have been knocked out in the collision, too!"

"Not if he expected me to panic and pile us up against one of the parked cars," Frank pointed out. "He'd have escaped, but we'd be in the hospital."

"And off the spy case!" Joe followed his brother's theory. "In other words, he may be a suspect!"

"Sure. He might be in cahoots with Hunter! We'd better let Mr. Wickerson know about this!"

Frank went back into the Pentagon and called from a pay phone. When Wickerson answered, the young detective described the near accident in South Parking and explained why he and Joe suspected Olson.

"Archie!" Wickerson exclaimed. "I would never have thought it of him. But you can bet I'll keep an eye on him from now on. Thanks for the tip."

Frank rejoined Joe, and they drove through Washington into Maryland. Heading due east, they came to Chesapeake Crossing down Chesapeake Bay from Annapolis.

The Sunset Motel was a medium-sized establishment made up of an office and a series of cabins along the shore. The Hardys registered and received the key to the last cabin of the group. They were stashing their belongings in the closet, when the phone rang.

Fenton Hardy's voice came over urgently, "I'll see you tomorrow!" Then he hung up abruptly.

117

"Uh-oh," Frank said. "Dad must be in a tight spot. He couldn't talk!"

"Do you know where he called from?"

"I have no idea."

"What do you think we should do?"

Frank shrugged. "He said he'd see us tomorrow. There's no point for us to stay here now. Let's have dinner and case the town."

"Okay."

The boys stopped at the motel diner for a quick meal, then went into Chesapeake Crossing. It was a typical town on the bay, with a long dock from which they could see boats bobbing up and down in the distance beneath a blue sky and fleecy white clouds overhead. Two headlands, on either side, protected a fishing fleet riding the gentle swell of the bay. Small craft were tied to the dock or anchored just out from it—rowboats, sailboats, motorboats, and houseboats.

Chelski's Marina occupied one end of the dock. Here boats were drawn up on land for scraping, painting, and repairs. Cars and barrels of bait lined the walls of the marina. Fishing boots, tackle, and crab nets were visible through the window.

"This is where Clifford Hunter was last seen," Frank commented. "Let's check it out."

The owner of the marina was a man named Herb Chelski. As the bell on the door announced the entry of the Hardys, he looked up from a crab net he was inspecting on the counter.

"What kind of boat do you want?" he inquired. "I have boats for the bay and the deep sea, and any kind of fishing boat you can mention. Except whale fishing," he added with a laugh. "If you're after Moby Dick, forget it."

"We're not after Moby Dick," Frank told him. "We're after Clifford Hunter."

Chelski stopped laughing. "Oh, the navy guy who disappeared. I told the FBI everything I know."

"We're cooperating with the FBI," Joe stated. "We're working for the Pentagon."

The Hardys produced their credentials, which Chelski scrutinized carefully. "Okay," he said finally. "I'll tell you how it was. Hunter owns a sailboat that he keeps docked here. He rents the space by the month. I got to know him pretty well. I thought he was a nice guy. What's he done?"

"I wish we could tell you," Frank replied. "But we can't. It's top-secret navy stuff."

"I understand. Well, I was here when Cliff came for his sailboat. He surprised me because it was a weekday and he usually takes his boat out on weekends. Besides, there was something funny about him this time."

"In what way?" Joe inquired.

"He didn't seem to be himself—acted nervous, if you know what I mean. But it didn't affect his sailing. He handled the boat as expertly as ever."

"And that was the last you saw of him?" Frank wanted to know.

"Yes. When he didn't come back, I figured he was on one of his longer trips down the bay. But when the FBI started asking questions, I realized Cliff was in some kind of trouble."

"Can you give us a description of Hunter's sailboat?"

"Sure. A thirty-three footer with a sail, and a motor for emergencies. The name *Bay Queen* is painted in green letters on the stern."

"I'd like to write down his address, too," Joe said. Chelski gave it to him, then the boys left the marina and strolled down the dock.

"I can understand why Hunter was nervous," Joe commented. "I'd be nervous too if I had just stolen a top-secret document from the navy."

Frank suddenly gripped Joe's arm. "Look there!" He pointed to a small, wizened figure walking along the dock ahead of them.

"Ed Bryle!" Joe marveled. "Where did he come from?"

"He doesn't know we're here. Let's brace him."

The Hardys applied their detective training to capturing their suspect. Joe stayed on Bryle's trail to make sure they would not lose him. Frank slipped around the dock and stepped out in front of the former farmhand. Joe at the same time closed in from the rear.

Bryle started when he saw Frank. He turned as if to run, but Joe was too near for him to get away.

"Hello, Bryle!" Frank said.

"Long time no see," Joe added.

Bryle flushed red and blinked his eyes. His voice shook. "What do you guys want?"

"A few answers," Frank replied. "What are you doing in Chesapeake Crossing?"

Bryle looked sullen. "I work at the marina. You got any complaints?"

"We heard you left the Hammerley farm," Joe stated.

"So? I got a better job here. Any objections?"

"Not as long as you return the *Galloping Rider*. Remember? The weather vane you snatched at Joshua Korbo's auction."

"You must be nuts!" Bryle snarled. "I wasn't at no auction."

"Come on, Bryle, we saw you!" Frank said. "You probably stole the *Galloping Rider* and hid it at the auction when Korbo wasn't looking. Then you came back to sneak it out during the bidding."

"And you only got away with it because the tent collapsed," Joe noted. "Otherwise we'd have collared you and returned the *Galloping Rider* to its owner. What have you done with it?"

"You can't prove a thing!" Bryle jeered. "Now let me go!"

Realizing he was right, the Hardys shrugged and Bryle smirked as he ambled down the dock.

"Too bad we can't blow the whistle on him," Frank said. "But we can always find him at the marina if we get any evidence against him that'll stand up."

The boys wandered around some more, then decided to take a boat out into the bay. Retracing their steps to the marina, they rented an outboard from Herb Chelski. They questioned him about Ed Bryle, and he said that Bryle was responsible for cleaning boats that had been rented and returned.

"Ed also brings boats to the dock when they're called for. He left one outboard tied to the dock. You can have it. Here are the keys."

Joe took the tiller as he and Frank chugged away from the dock and gained speed into Chesapeake Bay. Both were experienced sailors. They had their own motorboat back in Bayport called the *Sleuth*, which they cruised on Barmet Bay.

When they reached open water, they heard a roaring sound in the distance. The sound grew louder as it approached. A line of boats raced past, circled around a buoy, and zoomed up the other side.

"It's a race!" Frank shouted over the roar of

the motors. "I wish we had the *Sleuth* here to participate."

The last boat in the competition cut out too wide from the course and headed directly at them. Its propellers were low in the water, and its hull slapped the waves as it came. A youth about their age clung to the tiller, struggling to keep his boat on course. A couple of girls were perched on the seat watching him.

"I hope he has his boat under control!" said Joe.

"He doesn't," Frank warned. "Get ready for a maneuver to port!"

The other craft was almost upon them. Joe threw his weight against the tiller in a violent swing to the right. His outboard barely cleared the other boat as the girls giggled and waved at the Hardys. Spray deluged Frank and Joe, who heard the boy yell, "Sorry!" as he careened past them toward the buoy.

"Why don't you learn how to handle a boat!" Frank muttered, wiping the water from his eyes.

As dusk was falling, the brothers returned their boat to the marina and went back to their motel cabin. Half an hour later they heard a series of soft taps on the door. Frank positioned himself next to it against the wall, while Joe reluctantly turned the lock.

A man in ragged clothing, a scraggly beard, and bright red hair pushed past him into the room!

14

The Time Bomb

Frank grabbed the strange intruder around the shoulders as Joe kicked the door shut.

"Hold it!" said a familiar voice. "No need to be physical. But you could offer me a chair instead!"

"Dad!" the boys exclaimed in unison.

"Sh! Keep your voices down."

Frank looked puzzled. "You said you'd be here tomorrow."

"I had to say that in case the phone in this cabin is tapped. If someone listened in, he'll try to trap me tomorrow, and by that time I'll be gone."

"What's up?" Joe inquired.

"Joseph Wickerson relayed a warning from the FBI that foreign agents are on my trail. That's why I'm using this disguise and barged in on you without warning. Now fill me in on the Hammerley weather vane case."

The boys described their experiences at the farm, at Juniper Field, and in the town. They mentioned the weird, squeaky voice that threatened them over the phone, and told about encountering Ed Bryle, first at the auction, then in Chesapeake Crossing.

Frank concluded, "We haven't found a clue to connect Chesapeake Crossing and the paper with the Hammerley hex sign we discovered in the chopper at Juniper Field."

"Perhaps you should put the weather vanes on the back burner for the time being," Mr. Hardy said thoughtfully. "I could use you on the Pentagon spy mystery. I suppose Wickerson brought you up to date on the facts?"

"Yes," Frank said and told his father about their suspicion of Archie Olson.

Mr. Hardy stroked his chin quizzically. "I checked Olson out," he said, "and he came up clean. Of course, I may have missed a piece of incriminating evidence. Anyway, if Wickerson has him under surveillance, he won't be able to do any more damage."

He stood up and paced about the room. "Clifford Hunter is our real problem. To begin with, he hasn't left the country with the navy document. The CIA is quite certain, because if the foreign power involved had received the sub plan, it would have taken certain measures, like jamming our maser beams, for instance. Our monitoring devices show this hasn't been done.

"The danger is that Hunter might get out of the country at any time. The airports and shipping lines are being watched, and our government has special patrols on duty along the borders. So Hunter is probably lying low until the heat's off."

Frank spoke up. "Since he was last seen in Chesapeake Crossing, perhaps he's hiding not far from here. The bay's a great place to disappear. Lots of coves and inlets where a crook could hole up and nobody'd be the wiser."

Fenton Hardy nodded. "My thoughts exactly. Chesapeake Bay is so big, even the navy and the FBI haven't been able to look everywhere between Baltimore in the north and Norfolk in the south. My hunch is that Hunter hasn't gone any farther."

"So what's our next step?" Joe asked.

"I'll investigate by land to the south of Chesapeake Crossing while you two cruise in a powerboat along the shore. If we don't see any sign of Hunter or his sailboat, we'll try the north side."

"Good idea. When do we start?"

"Tomorrow morning. You know what the sailboat looks like. Here's a picture of Hunter."

He handed over a photograph. It portrayed a youngish man with brown hair and eyes and a moody expression. Frank and Joe examined it closely, then Frank slipped it into his pocket.

"We got Hunter's address from Mr. Chelski," Joe said. "Do you think it would be worthwhile to question the neighbors?"

"I've done that already. And the government has searched his apartment thoroughly and contacted practically everyone he knew. All we came up with is that he was known to be a nice guy, who liked to read and sail. No suspicious traits or acquaintances. That's what makes this case so difficult."

Mr. Hardy stood up. "I'll keep in touch with you through this motel. And now I'd better leave, but I don't want to use the door. Someone may be watching it."

He went to an open window at the back of the room, climbed quickly and silently over the sill, and dropped to the ground. Seconds later he had vanished amid the shrubbery into the darkness of the night.

Early the next morning, Frank and Joe walked back to Chelski's Marina, where they found Herb Chelski going over his list of customers for the day.

"We'd like to hire a powerboat," Frank said.

"I've got just what you want," Chelski replied and went to the door. "Ed, bring the small cabin cruiser up to the landing. It's for Frank and Joe

127

Hardy." He turned back to the boys. "Go on down. I'll be there in a few minutes."

At the landing the boys saw a sleek powerboat approaching. Ed Bryle was at the wheel. Putting the motor in idle, he jumped onto the dock with a rope in his hand.

"Okay, fellows," he said in a friendly manner. "The boat's all yours."

Frank and Joe got in and Bryle tossed the rope onto the deck. Then he pushed the hull away from the landing. Frank shifted into gear and the boat moved off.

"What's come over Bryle?" he wondered. "He's so friendly all of a sudden."

"Probably didn't want his boss to know that we've met before and under what circumstances," Joe guessed.

They rounded one of the Chesapeake Crossing headlands and cruised along the shore, which was indented by coves and inlets, some small enough to be inspected from deep water, others requiring a closer approach.

Joe sighed. "This is like looking for a needle in a haystack," he said, trying to shield his eyes from the burning sun.

"Or a flounder in Chesapeake Bay," Frank added. "Boy, it's getting hot!"

They came to an inlet so protected by underbrush and overhanging trees that the interior could not be viewed from their boat. "That would be a good place to hide," Frank observed. "Let's go in."

He steered his craft into the inlet. Birds rose in raucous protest at the sound of their engine, but otherwise there was no sign of life. The inlet extended for a few hundred yards, then, reaching the end, Frank turned back for the open bay.

They scouted inlet after inlet, eating the sandwiches Joe had brought in lieu of breakfast without ever taking their eyes off the coastline. Finally something caught Joe's eye on the way out of a small cove. Leaning over the side of their boat, he plucked a life preserver from the water, inspected it, and cried out, "Frank! Look at this!" He pointed at the faded words on the side of the life preserver: *Bay Queen*. "This is from Hunter's sailboat. He's been here, and maybe he still is!"

They scouted all around the small cove but found no trace of the fugitive.

"The life preserver might have floated in here from somewhere else," Frank noted. "Let's go on farther down the bay."

Leaving the cove, they continued south. A sailboat moved across their bow in the distance. It was about thirty feet long, with a red band along the waterline. As it turned, Joe saw the word *Queen* in green letters on the stern.

"It's the *Bay Queen!*" he shouted.

Frank swerved toward the sailboat and gained speed. They closed in rapidly. A man glared at them from the deck. "What are you trying to do," he shouted, "cause an accident?"

"I'll call the Coast Guard," Joe offered.

"Wait a minute," Frank said. They had reached the stern of the craft and shot beyond it. He looked back and read the full name of the sailboat: *Chesapeake Queen.*

"I don't think the Coast Guard would have been interested in her," he pointed out with a chuckle. Crestfallen, his brother agreed.

After another hour, the boys began to feel hungry again. Joe took a fishing rod from a closet in the cabin, dropped a line in the water, and within minutes landed a mess of Chesapeake Bay perch. A stove in the small galley enabled him to fry his catch, and they found fresh bottled water to drink with their fish.

Then Joe took the wheel while Frank cleaned up the galley. They paused for an inspection of an inlet whenever the possibilities appeared good. But their quest was in vain. Glumly, Frank stared at their wake as they chugged along doggedly. Suddenly he called out, "Hey, Joe! I think we missed a cove. The entrance is almost hidden, but I just caught a glimpse of it."

Joe went into reverse and they came to a deep sandy cove with a mouth almost too narrow for their motorboat to pass through. Shrubs and large rocks all but hid the inlet from view.

"Better shut the engine off and drift in," Frank advised. "Otherwise we might hit those rocks."

Joe cut the motor and both boys grabbed paddles. Slowly and carefully they made their way through the narrow mouth of the cove. On the other side, amid the surrounding foliage, they could make out the dim shape of a sailboat rocking in the waves some distance away.

"That could be the *Bay Queen!*" Frank said excitedly. "Joe, get the binoculars!"

The younger Hardy produced a pair from a locker and focused on the sailboat. "We'll have to go in for a close-up," he decided. "I can't read anything from here."

He handed the glasses to Frank, who took a quick look and confirmed Joe's opinion. "But I don't want to pile us up on those rocks," he said. "The whole cove is full of them."

They were discussing the best way of maneuvering their powerboat, when the silence of the inlet was broken by an intermittent sound like that of a clock. Immersed in their problem of navigating into the cove, the boys at first had not noticed the ticking.

131

"Frank—what *is* that?" Joe stared at his brother in puzzlement. "Sounds like a clock. With the engine running, we didn't hear it before."

He stared at the dashboard, but the sound came from the engine compartment. Suddenly the truth hit both boys at the same time.

"There's a time bomb on board!" Frank yelled. "And it may go off any second!"

15

The Bay Queen

The Hardys dived over the side of the cabin cruiser simultaneously. Plunging into the water, they swam beneath the surface for several yards, then rose as their lungs began to pound for air. They moved away from the powerboat as fast as they could.

Only seconds later, the time bomb exploded! With a deafening sound, it tore their craft apart. Fragments arched high into the air and fell back into the water. Heavy bits of wood and metal splashed near Frank and Joe, who turned to see the results of the shattering explosion.

Soon there was only an oil slick where the power-boat had been. Life jackets and seat cushions float-ed on the surface next to fishing rods, floppy straw hats, and splinters from the hull.

Unharmed by the flying debris, Frank began to tread water. "Are you okay?" he called to Joe.

"I banged my knee when I went over the side, but it's just a bruise."

Together they swam to the rocks and clambered out of the water. They lay there, panting heavily, until their strength returned.

"Good thing we switched the engine off," Joe said. "Otherwise we wouldn't have heard the ticking of the clock!"

"Ed Bryle must have planted that time bomb," Frank said grimly. "He's the only one with a motive. He could have done it when he was getting the boat ready for us!"

"That's why he was so friendly," Joe added. "He thought we were headed for the bottom of the bay. We'll fix his wagon when we get back to Chesapeake Crossing!"

They sat up and looked around the cove. The sailboat was clearly visible now. It had swung around in the tide, and the words *Bay Queen* were written in large letters on the stern. However, there was no sign of anyone aboard.

Frank and Joe rose to their feet and stepped carefully toward the shore from rock to rock. Jumping into the sand, they circled around the cove through the underbrush, maneuvering as silently as possible because they could not be sure Hunter was

134

not around. On the edge of the beach, they parted the tall grass and peered through at the *Bay Queen.*

The sailboat rode freely in the water. It was neither anchored nor tied to a tree to keep it from drifting off. Its sail was still up, and a wind off Chesapeake Bay made the craft rock from side to side.

"She wasn't sailed in here," Frank whispered. "I'll bet she drifted in from the bay!"

"Let's split up and approach from different directions anyway," Joe cautioned. "We don't want to take any chances."

Frank nooded and they cautiously moved out of the underbrush across the sand and waded through the water to opposite ends of the sailboat.

Frank climbed aboard at the bow, Joe at the stern. Quietly they descended the steps into the cabin. Both were ready for action if Hunter happened to be there, but they found the cabin empty.

Searching for clues, they discovered the ownership papers in a drawer under the front window. They were made out in the name of Clifford Hunter.

"That makes it official," Joe said.

"But it doesn't tell us where Hunter is," Frank replied. "Keep going!"

A few minutes later, the younger Hardy pointed to a wooden seat under a side porthole. "Look at this!" he said. Scratched in crude, scrawling letters in the paint of the seat were the words "Barren Island."

"Any idea what it means?" Frank asked.

"No. Maybe it's an island in Chesapeake Bay."

"We'd better check. But first we'll have to get this sailboat back to town so the FBI can go over it."

"Right. But how about drying out a little first? I feel clammy."

Frank and Joe went up on deck and sat in the sun until their clothes felt comfortable, when suddenly they heard the putt-putting of a motorboat beyond the trees. Then the boat stopped and an anchor splashed into the water.

The Hardys could not see who was in the craft, but they prepared to conceal themselves in case it was Clifford Hunter returning for his sailboat. Before they could move, they heard a loud splashing not far from the rocks. A tenor voice began to sing a rousing sea chantey.

"That can't be Hunter," Joe murmured. "Wherever he is, he'd hardly draw attention to himself."

"Right. But let's see who it is, anyway."

They jumped from the sailboat onto the sand and retraced their steps stealthily through the woods back to the rocks. A large boulder gave them cover from which to look down into the water. They saw the anchored motorboat with a man wading near it.

"Gaspard Clay!" Frank exclaimed in astonishment. The curator of the county historical museum, dressed in white nautical garb, wore a broad straw hat that flopped down over his ears. Protected by hip boots, he stepped through the water with a crab net drawn back across his shoulder like a baseball bat. He sang so loudly that it seemed deafening to the Hardys at such close range.

Every so often Clay swung his net down and drew it up leaking water and sand. If he had caught a crab, he dumped it into a large pot in his motorboat. Frank and Joe could not help laughing at the sight of Gaspard Clay out after crab.

"No point in hiding from him," Joe said.

Frank nodded. "But let's not tell him anything. He'll talk, and everyone in Chesapeake Crossing will know we're on the spy case. I'd prefer he not see the *Bay Queen*, either."

"Right."

The boys left the cover of the boulder and walked down onto the beach. Clay smiled when he saw them.

"This is quite a surprise," he declared. "How, ahem, do you boys happen to be here?"

"We took your advice," Joe said. "Went sailing on the bay. How's the crabbing?"

"Excellent! As I told you, best there is! I had a day off at the museum, so I came down here." As he spoke, he produced two more crab nets from his boat. "Will you boys join me?"

The Hardys exchanged glances. It would be one way to keep Clay from discovering the *Bay Queen*. Besides, they enjoyed crabbing, something they often did at home in Barmet Bay.

Taking off their shoes and socks and rolling up their pants legs, they each took a net from Clay and accompanied him through the water along the shoreline. They made sure to take a direction away from the cove where the sailboat lay. Clay offered no objection because the crabs were abundant everywhere.

"Ouch!" Frank exclaimed suddenly.

"Is something, ahem, the matter?" Clay inquired.

In reply, Frank lifted his foot clear of the water and revealed a crab clinging to his big toe. Gingerly he released his toe and tossed the offending crustacean into the pot.

"That's a smart way to catch a crab!" Joe kidded his brother.

Frank grimaced. "All right, wise guy. I didn't expect any sympathy!"

Clay finally decided their catch was big enough. "You boys caught some of the crabs," he said. "How about helping me, ahem, dispose of some? Eat them, I mean."

"That sounds great!" Joe said. "Too bad Chet isn't here."

They started for shore and Clay transferred a number of crabs from his big pot to a smaller one. Then he led the way to the beach. Frank and Joe gathered driftwood for a fire, and soon the water in the pot began to boil. Clay cooked the crabs, and the three had a hearty dinner sitting on the sand.

Afterward, Clay told them he had to return to Chesapeake Crossing. "I'm due, ahem, in the museum tomorrow. Want a ride to the marina? There's room for three in my motorboat."

"No thanks," Frank said casually. "We're moored farther south."

Clay nodded, caroled another chantey, and chugged off with a smile and a wave of his hand.

Frank and Joe returned to the *Bay Queen*. After thoroughly inspecting it, they decided it was seaworthy. Using the motor, Frank backed the sailboat away from the sand, turned it around, and guided it between the rocks out into Chesapeake Bay. A wind was rising.

"Let's try the sail," Joe suggested. "This wind'll give us as much speed as the motor."

Frank cut off the power while Joe took control of the sail, and they swiftly scudded over the waves. Later they changed places, with Frank guiding the sailboat through the wind and spray of the bay.

At last Chesapeake Crossing appeared over their bow. Frank edged the *Bay Queen* up to the landing of Chelski's Marina, and Joe leaped ashore with one

139

end of a rope, which he looped around a stanchion to hold the boat in place.

Then they went to find Herb Chelski. He was in his office.

"I'm afraid your powerboat is gone," Frank said.

"If you hit a rock and the boat sank, you'll have to pay for it!" Chelski growled.

"It didn't sink. It went up in the air."

"Come again?"

"It had a time bomb aboard and almost killed us!" Joe declared. "We escaped just before it went off."

"What!" Chelski stared at him in disbelief.

"We think Ed Bryle planted the bomb," Frank added. "You see, we know he stole a valuable antique in Pennsylvania Dutch country and he wanted us out of the way."

"We'd like to talk to him," Joe added.

"Ed isn't here anymore!" Chelski exploded. "He quit his job just after you two left this morning." He looked greatly disturbed and ran his fingers through his hair in agitation. "Look, fellows, I'm awfully sorry. I'll have Ed Bryle prosecuted for attempted murder if he turns up again. But I hope you realize I had nothing to do with it—"

"Don't worry, Mr. Chelski," Frank assured him. "We know you didn't. But you must understand that we can't be responsible for the boat under the circumstances, either."

"Of course." Chelski seemed relieved.

"We found Clifford Hunter's sailboat," Joe said, changing the subject. "It was in a cove down Chesapeake Bay."

"You're kidding! You mean Cliff came back with you?"

Joe shook his head. "No. We have no idea where he is. The boat was abandoned. We tied it to your dock. Can you make sure it's kept as is until the FBI checks it out?"

"Sure," Chelski promised. "I won't let anyone touch it."

The Hardys said good-bye to the marina owner and returned to the Sunset Motel, where the desk clerk handed them a small package, about four by six inches and rather flat.

"I don't know who delivered it," he said. "I was away from the desk showing a guest to his room. When I got back, this package was here with your names on it."

Joe picked it up. It was lightweight. "Thanks," he said, and the boys went to their cabin. Frank immediately called the FBI in Washington. When he mentioned Clifford Hunter's name, he was shifted by intercom to the office of the director, who listened with intense interest to the story of the *Bay Queen.*

"You boys have done great work," he praised

141

them. "This is the first real break we've had on the case. An FBI agent will leave Washington for Chesapeake Crossing at once."

While Frank was making the phone call, Joe unwrapped the package. It was a cassette!

"There's a player in the lobby," Frank said after he hung up. "Let's try it."

The boys went to the machine that stood in one corner of the room. No one was there. Frank turned the player on after slipping the cassette into place.

Seconds went by, and they heard nothing but the slight rustling of the spool revolving.

"Nothing on it," Joe said finally.

"Must be a hoax," Frank agreed. He was about to remove the cassette when the silence was broken.

"Hardys, the hex is on you!" squealed the strange voice that had threatened them before. "Get off the case or you'll be playing tag with the crabs at the bottom of the bay!"

16

Barren Island Hideout

Startled, the boys let the tape continue in case there was more to the threat. However, the tape finished playing in silence. Frank turned the cassette over. The other side was blank, too. He took the tape out of the player and put it in his pocket. "Whoever this weirdo is," he said, "he's warning us off the case. I just wonder which one he means, the Pentagon spy case or the weather vane mystery?"

"Must be the weather vane investigation," Joe said. " He threatened us once before when we were still at Hammerley's to beware of the hex. At that time we weren't even working on the Pentagon spy mystery."

"Which means he trailed us here all the way from Pennsylvania Dutch country," Frank concluded. "We'd better make sure he doesn't follow us to Barren Island, or he might interfere with our work for Dad!"

"Right. That's our next project. Let's get a map and see if we can find the place."

Frank bought a nautical chart of Chesapeake Bay, then they went to their cabin. The phone rang as they walked in the door. The caller was their father, who asked them to go to a public booth and call him back so they could talk without being overheard by a potential wiretapper.

Frank and Joe went to the nearest diner and were soon speaking to the detective, telling him the news. When he heard about their discovery of Clifford Hunter's sailboat, he was elated.

"This gives us something to go on!" he exclaimed. "And it shows my theory was right about Hunter staying in this area. I'll keep looking for him on land; you follow up the Barren Island angle. It's near the Eastern Shore of Maryland."

Then he hung up and the boys returned to their room. They consulted their chart of Chesapeake Bay. Finding that Barren Island lay nearly opposite the mouth of the Potomac River, they plotted the best course from Chesapeake Crossing.

In the morning they rented another powerboat from Herb Chelski at the marina. They made sure no one was following them, then cruised to Barren Island. Edging up to the beach, they tied their boat to a small bush half hidden in the sand and went ashore.

The island was about a mile across. Sand and scrub vegetation met their eyes wherever they looked.

"Barren Island is the right name for this place. Who'd want to live here?" Joe said.

Frank pointed to a building on the opposite shore. "Somebody does. Even though it's hidden by those bushes, it looks like a big house. Let's check it out."

The boys rounded the island and pulled into a derelict wharf. The pilings that once formed steps leading up from the water had slipped into a jumbled heap. Climbing to the top, the Hardys found a walk made up of broken flagstones with weeds growing between them.

The house was in ramshackle condition. The windows were boarded up and shingles from the roof littered the ground. Most of the porch railings were broken, and birds nested in the chimney.

"I guess I was wrong," Frank said. "Nobody lives here. Looks as if the owners just sailed away and left the house to fall down."

Joe tried the front door. "It's locked," he said. Circling the house they found the back door locked as well. Joe scratched his head. "What do we do now? Break a window?"

"Let's check the cellar door first," Frank suggested, and they went to the wooden doors covering the entrance to the basement. Frank lifted one. It rose on creaking hinges and hung partway open. "It's too rusty to lie flat," he said. Descending the stone steps, he tried the handle to the cellar door. "It's open," he called in a muted tone to his brother. "Come on."

The boys went into the basement. It was clothed in semidarkness because the boarded windows let in only a few rays of light. A musty smell greeted them, the result of the house being boarded up for years. Water oozed through cracks in the foundation and lay in puddles on the flagstones of the floor.

"Nice home for rats!" Joe muttered as a rodent scurried out from underfoot.

The boys scouted through the cellar, poking around piles of torn fishnet, broken oars, and clamshells. "Look at this!" Frank said with a low chuckle. He held up a bow and arrow. "Chet should be here."

Joe grinned. "He'd try crabbing with it!"

Frank tossed the bow and arrow aside, and they went deeper into the cellar until they came to a second room in the back, where a flight of stairs led to the first floor. They could make out a number of barrels in the semidarkness.

Joe squatted on his heels. "Flour, sugar, salt," he read in large letters on the barrels. "This must have been the storage room. The other—"

A loud noise at the cellar door brought him to his feet. "Somebody's at the rear door!" he cried.

In a flash, both boys raced back through the basement toward the steps leading outside. The wooden doors were back in place over their heads!

"We're locked in!" Joe gasped.

Frank pressed his hand against one door and breathed a sigh of relief. "It's open," he said. "The wind must have closed it."

"Thank goodness!" Joe blurted out. "I really got scared for a minute."

"Me too!"

They returned to the cellar and Joe stopped at the stack of fishing rods. "Hey, Frank! I don't see the bow and arrow anymore. You think someone took them?"

Frank shook his head. "I tossed them aside and they probably got stuck in those nets. It's too dark to look for them. We've got to go through the rest of the house, so let's not waste time."

Passing through the cellar, they reached the stairs and went up to the first floor. The kitchen was large with an old-fashioned wood-burning stove. Kindling protruded from the top of a barrel next to it, and there were fragments of broken dishes on the counter.

"Do you figure anyone's been cooking on the stove lately?" Frank asked.

147

Joe drew a line through the dust between two burners. "Not since the year one." He lifted a heavy lid and looked inside. "Nothing but old ashes," he announced.

The dining room was empty except for a chair with a broken leg. They went into a hall flanking the living room, which was equally bare. A board had fallen from the picture window in front, admitting a broad shaft of sunlight. The fireplace was boarded up, and dust covered everything.

"Nothing in there," Joe said, after peering in from the hall. "Let's go upstairs."

The bedrooms on the second floor contained no furniture, either, and the boys drew a blank on possible clues. They proceeded to the attic, a low-ceilinged room up against the roof. Eight-by-fours formed two catwalks across the beams on opposite ends, which slanted down so sharply from the peak of the roof that the boys had to move part of the way on their hands and knees.

Frank took one catwalk and Joe the other. The ceiling was stained in many places by rain leaking through holes in the roof. A bird fled from its nest on one windowsill as Joe approached. They saw nothing except pieces of tar paper strewn about.

"Nothing here but the pigeons," Frank said, coughing from the dust. "They can have it. I'm getting out!"

"I'll race you to the door," Joe said with a grin.

They crawled along the catwalks to the attic door, emerged, and stretched their cramped muscles. Then they descended the stairs to the ground floor.

In the hallway, Joe expressed his disappointment. "We bombed again! Took that long trip over here for nothing!"

Frank had been staring at the floor. "Wait a minute!" he exclaimed suddenly. "Look here!"

He pointed to marks in the dust at the front door. "Here's a footprint. A lot of footprints!"

Joe was galvanized by the sight. "You're right! Let's see where they go."

The Hardys followed the trail through the hall into the living room and up to the fireplace. The prints became indistinct there in front of the boards covering the opening, as if someone had moved about in that particular area of the room.

"Somebody's been here!" Frank declared. "And there's a trail leading back to the front door!"

Joe dropped onto one knee and inspected the marks more closely. "There are *four* sets of prints coming in, but only *three* going out!" he declared.

Frank nodded grimly. "Something peculiar's been going on here. We'll have to—"

Wham! Something zipped across the room and slammed into one of the boards covering the fireplace. Looking up, the boys saw an arrow quivering in the wood just above their heads!

17

The Captive

Whirling around, the Hardys spotted a shadow flitting past outside the picture window.

"Let's get him!" Joe shouted.

They ran to the window and peered through the opening where the board had fallen down. On the ground outside lay the bow Frank had discovered in the cellar. They saw a tall man wearing a black beard and dark glasses running toward the beach!

"That's our suspect!" Joe cried. "The guy who rented the chopper from Juniper Field!"

Without another word, the Hardys hurled themselves against the remaining boards in the window, which gave way and clattered to the ground. Frank and Joe vaulted through the opening, landed in the sand, and ran after him.

They rapidly closed the gap between themselves

and the fugitive, who was running toward an outboard motorboat pulled up on the beach. Frank leaped through the air and hit the man with a flying tackle just before he reached the water's edge. They went down in a heap and rolled over and over in the sand, struggling furiously.

Frank was about to pin his antagonist as in a wrestling match, when suddenly the man reached into his pocket, pulled out a blackjack, and struck the boy on the side of his head. Dizzily, Frank fell into the sand.

Joe had rushed up and grappled with the fugitive, but he too suffered a blow from the blackjack that broke his grip. In a flash, the man dashed away.

Momentarily stunned, the Hardys pulled themselves up on their hands and knees, shaking their heads to clear the cobwebs. They heard the putt-putt of the motorboat racing away from the island. Quickly they rose and dashed to the beach, but now the boat was safely out of their reach.

"No use trying to catch him," Joe said in disgust. "He could be in Baltimore by the time we get our boat. Say, are you okay, Frank?"

"Just a bruise," his brother replied, feeling a tender spot where the blackjack had struck. "I'll live. How about you?"

"Same. He only hit me a glancing blow. Anyhow, we know he followed us into the cellar and took the bow and arrow. When he fired the arrow from the window, he was trying to frighten us away from the house—"

"Which means something's in there he doesn't want us to see!" Frank inferred excitedly. "Maybe Hammerley's weather vane's hidden in the place. We'll have to find out. Come on!"

The boys climbed back into the house through the picture window and retraced their steps to the fireplace. Just then they heard a low groan from behind the boards covering the opening!

"Someone's in there!" Frank cried out. He attacked one of the boards, wrenching it loose. Joe took another. Within seconds they had the fireplace cleared.

A man lay in a crumpled heap inside!

The Hardys lifted him into the living room and peered curiously at his face.

"He looks familiar," Frank muttered, trying to recognize the man through the stubble of his beard. He pulled the photograph of Clifford Hunter out of his pocket and studied it, comparing it with the man in front of them.

"That's him!" he gasped. "Joe, we've found the Pentagon spy!"

"He's been drugged," Joe said. "I'll see if I can bring him around." He took a small vial of smelling salts from his pocket detective kit and held it under Hunter's nose. The stricken man began to move convulsively. Gradually, however, his heavy breathing subsided to its normal rate. He opened his eyes and focused them on the Hardys. "Who are you?" he asked weakly.

"We'll tell you later," Frank promised. "First you need some fresh air."

He and Joe carried the man through the front door and set him down in the sand, leaning him against a rock. A breeze blowing off Chesapeake Bay cleared the captive's head. Then the boys introduced themselves.

"We've been looking for you," Frank informed him.

Hunter was puzzled. "Why? I don't even know you."

"The Pentagon wants us to get back the navy plan you stole," Joe explained.

"I didn't steal it," Hunter protested. "I took the document, but I didn't steal it."

"What do you mean?" Joe queried.

"Joe Wickerson told me to take it. Later I realized that he had slipped me a mind-altering drug—"

"Wickerson!" Frank exploded. "You mean to say your boss in the navy is the real Pentagon spy?"

Hunter nodded. "I'll explain. But first tell me what you know. It'll make it easier." He was very weak, and speaking was an effort for him.

Quickly the Hardys told about their visit to the

Pentagon and their interview with Joseph Wickerson. They added their suspicion of Archie Olson, who had almost run them over in the parking lot.

"Olson had nothing to do with the theft," Hunter said. "But he's a terrible driver."

The boys grinned. "He sure is," Frank said.

Hunter took a deep breath. "Wickerson didn't catch me in the files of the Cosmo Rocket. I caught him. I had clearance, and he didn't. That made me suspicious of him, and he knew it.

"Shortly afterward, I saw him pouring a white powder into my coffee. He said it was sugar, but since then I've learned that it wasn't. I'm not a spy, but I took the MASUB plan because Wickerson had me in his power!"

"He told you to remove the plan from the files?" Frank asked.

"Yes. He gave me instructions to take it to Chesapeake Crossing, where I kept my sailboat. He knew about that because he's been aboard on some of my cruises."

Hunter paused a few moments to rest, then went on: "Joe laid a trap for me. I got only a few miles out into the bay when a powerboat cut across my bow and made me heave to. Three men with guns came aboard the *Bay Queen*. Apparently Wickerson had told them where I would be."

"Did you recognize the men?" Joe inquired.

"No, I never saw them before. One was a short,

wizened fellow who dressed like a farmhand."

"Ed Bryle!" Joe exclaimed. "The guy Hammerley fired!"

"Who's Hammerley?" Hunter asked, puzzled.

"A farmer from Pennsylvania. Ed Bryle went to work at Chelski's Marina afterward and blew our boat up with a time bomb. Can you tell us more about the other two men who held you up?"

Hunter tapped his thumb against his chin. "Well, one of them was called Crow by the other two."

Frank gasped. "That must be Crow Morven, the foreman at Hammerley's farm who also tried to get us out of the way!"

"Your life must have been in great danger," Hunter said worriedly.

"That's part of detective work," Frank said. "Can you tell us anything about the third man?"

"He was tall, had a black beard, and wore dark glasses."

"That's the guy who just tried to hit us with an arrow!" Joe declared. "I wish you could identify him by name."

Hunter shook his head. "Sorry, but I can't help you with that. I'd recognize his voice; and the only other thing I noticed was that his beard looked, well, sort of plastic."

"It must be phony," Joe commented. "Part of his disguise. The dark glasses are, too."

"What did the men do after they boarded your sailboat?" Frank asked.

"Blackbeard took the MASUB blueprint from me. Then he ordered the others to lock me in the cabin. I could hear them talk about their plans up on deck."

"Good! What did they say?" Frank urged.

"I discovered Wickerson is a spy scheming to sell the MASUB document to a foreign power. They laughed about the way he had used his mind-altering drug on me and made me steal the plan. I was scheduled to be the fall guy," Hunter added bitterly.

"Did you scratch the words 'Barren Island' into the bench of your sailboat?" Frank asked.

Hunter nodded. "My captors mentioned that they were bringing me here, where they intended to hold me and make me tell them everything I knew about the navy's nuclear submarine program. If I wouldn't cooperate they said they would sink me into the bay."

The exhausted scientist fell silent for a moment, and the Hardys mulled over his story. Finally Joe asked whether Hunter had heard the men say anything else.

"Yes, strangely enough they mentioned weather vanes!"

18

The Horse Thieves

Frank jumped up excitedly. "So there's a connection between our two cases after all!" he exclaimed.

"What do you mean?" Hunter asked, baffled.

Frank told him about their investigation of the stolen antiques. "What exactly did your captors say about weather vanes?" he inquired.

"That they had a lucrative business going with them. They had a code system based on hex signs," Hunter explained. "The weather vanes they picked out were identified by the hex sign on the building from which each one was to be lifted. I also heard the men mentioning a weather vane called the *Galloping Rider* and that it was going to the Korbo auction."

Frank nodded. "We saw it there. But we thought the fence was in Chesapeake Crossing."

"It is," Hunter replied. "But they routed the antiques through different channels. For instance, they said that the *Flashing Arrow* was not sent directly to the fence, either, because those boys from Bayport had poked their noses into the business."

Hunter shifted weakly in the sand. "That's all I can tell you. I heard nothing more. Do you have any idea where my sailboat is?"

Frank told him that the boys had found it and returned it to Chelski's Marina.

"Oh, I'm glad," Hunter said. "She's a fine boat. I'd hate to lose her."

"What happened when your captors brought you to Barren Island?" Joe queried.

"They gave me another dose of the drug, but this time it was weaker, and when they tried to pump me about navy secrets I was able to remain quiet. So they boarded me up in the fireplace. Told me I'd have plenty of time to think things over in solitary. Who knows, they might have let me die if you boys hadn't come along!"

Joe stood up. "You know, the man in the black glasses who shot an arrow at us before he took off in his motorboat—maybe he went to round up his buddies. We'd better get out of here. Will you be able to walk down to the beach, Mr. Hunter?"

"I think so." Hunter stood up but teetered dizzily. He leaned on the boys and they hurried to their powerboat as fast as they could. Minutes later they skimmed across Chesapeake Bay.

Night was falling when they returned to the marina. Herb Chelski had gone home, and the watchman who took the boat did not know Clifford Hunter. The boys were relieved, because they felt it would be best if Hunter had a chance to rest in their cabin before the FBI was notified.

When they arrived at the motel and walked into their room, Mr. Hardy was sitting in an easy chair. He stared at the trio in utter surprise.

"You found Clifford Hunter!" he called out and jumped up in excitement.

"Yes, Dad," Frank replied. "Mr. Hunter, this is our father. He was asked by the government to head the search for you."

Hunter smiled wearily and sank into a chair. He could hardly speak. While Joe went out to get some food for him, Frank quickly told his father what had happened.

"This matches with what I found out," Mr. Hardy said. "I had become suspicious of Wickerson because he seemed to hamper my investigation with false clues. But I needed to find Mr. Hunter to prove that Wickerson was the real Pentagon spy!"

He turned to the scientist. "I'm sorry you had to go through all this. I'll phone Washington right away and have your boss arrested."

Mr. Hardy made the call, and after he hung up, he smiled. "Joseph Wickerson was taken into custody an hour ago," he reported. "He was caught stealing a document from the Cosmo Rocket file."

Joe returned with a plate of food and hot coffee, and the scientist ate hungrily while the boys told their father about the weather vane connection.

"I'd like to call Mr. Hammerley and tell him what we learned," Frank said and went to the telephone. When he reached Hammerley, their friend was greatly alarmed.

"I saw Ed Bryle here today, and shortly afterward he and Morven rode off on two of my horses!" he sputtered. "Can you come back here and find them?"

"We'll be there in the morning, Mr. Hammerley," Frank promised. "We have an idea who the weather vane thieves are. They're tied in with a spy case our father's been investigating."

"Have you caught the gang?" the farmer asked hopefully.

"Not yet. But we will!"

The following morning, the boys drove to Pennsylvania, while Mr. Hardy and Clifford Hunter took an early flight to Washington. When the boys arrived at the Hammerley farm, their host told them what had happened.

"I found out that Morven had hidden Ed Bryle

on the farm overnight," he told the boys. "So I fired him on the spot. About an hour later they both rode off on my horses!"

"Bryle must have come here after he tried to blow us to smithereens with a time bomb on Chesapeake Bay," Frank said and reported their adventures to the farmer. When he repeated the conversation he had overheard taking place between Bryle, Morven, and the black-bearded man, Hammerley was stupefied.

"You mean Morven was plotting to steal my weather vane while I thought he was guarding it from the thieves?"

"That's right," Frank said. "And that's why he tried to get us off the case by playing mean and dangerous tricks on us."

"I wonder where he and Bryle went," Joe spoke up. "Do you have any idea, Mr. Hammerley?"

"The police asked the same thing when I phoned them about the horses. I told them I didn't know where the scoundrels had gone. I still don't know."

"Let's check the stable," Frank suggested. "We might find a clue there."

The Hardys left the house and walked past the barn. They looked up at the roof, which seemed bare now that the *Flashing Arrow* was not there any longer, turning in the wind.

The stable stood about one hundred yards from the barn in the direction of the pasture. It was made up of a series of stalls, from which horses stared through half-doors marked with their names. Two empty stalls with "Star" and "Bronco" on them showed where Morven and Bryle had obtained their mounts.

The boys entered the stable and walked along a wall hung with equestrian equipment. As expert riders who often cantered along bridle trails near Bayport, they eagerly examined saddles, boots, and horseshoes.

But the search was in vain. "I didn't expect them to leave a road map," Frank grumbled, "but after we found the paper in the chopper ..." his voice trailed off.

"I know what you mean," Joe said. "Too bad we weren't in luck this time."

After they reported their failure to Hammerley, Frank raised a question. "Why did Morven and Bryle take horses, not one of the cars? They could have made much better time in a car."

"Not if they were headed for town!" Joe exclaimed, seeing his brother's reasoning. "They went the shortest way—across the pasture and through the woods. A car couldn't get through, and they didn't want to lose time driving around the detour where the bridge is out!"

"That makes sense, young man," Hammerley agreed. "I'll call the police right away and tell them to look for those two crooks!"

He went to the phone and tried to get a connection. Then he replaced the instrument in its cradle with a despairing gesture. "The phone is dead!" he declared.

"Morven and Bryle must have cut the line," Joe guessed. "I just wish we knew where they went. They could be anywhere in town or even at one of the farms around it!"

The boys sat in glum silence trying to plan their next move. Suddenly Frank had an idea. "Mr. Hammerley, do you have a cassette player?"

"Sure I do. I record messages for the grain dealers all the time. Why do you ask?"

"I'd like to try something." Frank told Hammerley about the tape they had received at the Sunset Motel. "Mind if I play it again?" he asked.

"Of course not. Follow me."

When Hammerley heard the weird voice, he was puzzled. "Who in the world would talk like that?" he wondered.

"Is there a speed control on this machine?" Frank asked.

Hammerley showed him where it was, and the young detective turned it down. He replayed the tape, adjusting the speed even further. The voice diminished from the weird squeak to a normal range, and everyone gasped.

The speaker was Gaspard Clay!

19

Caught by the Enemy!

Frank and Joe stared at one another and Hammerley stood staring, his mouth open, as the cassette spun on to the end of its message.

"Gaspard Clay!" he gulped. "How did you know his voice was on the tape?"

"I didn't," Frank replied. "It just occurred to me suddenly that whoever made the recording might have changed the frequency to disguise his voice. When Joe and I experimented with tape recordings in our lab, we did that once."

"That's right," Joe added. "Lucky you thought of that, Frank. Say, I'll bet Clay made this recording right after we talked to him at the museum. When we asked him about Chesapeake Crossing, he must have figured we were headed there. So he warned us over the phone first, then took the cassette down there to try to scare us away."

"As long as Clay is one of the weather vane gang," Frank mused, "he's probably involved with the Pentagon spy, too."

"This is all very confusing," Hammerley said. "Why don't you bring me up to date on your investigation?"

Frank explained the connection of the two cases. "Morven and Bryle also worked for Wickerson," he said. "Since they went into town, they probably have joined Clay."

The light dawned on Joe. "The stolen weather vanes might be at the museum!" he exclaimed. "We'd better get over there fast before the gang moves the stuff out!"

"May we borrow two of your horses, Mr. Hammerley?" Frank asked.

"Sure. Take Red and King. They're the best saddle mounts I own."

The Hardys raced to the stable, took down bridles and saddles of burnished leather from pegs on the wall, and hurried into the stalls. Frank took Red, while Joe saddled King. Then they led the animals out of their stalls. The horses champed at the bit and pawed the ground as the boys mounted them.

Frank patted Red on the shoulder and tugged on the bridle. "Come on," he coaxed. "Let's see what you can do!"

The horse cantered a few steps then broke into a fast gallop. Joe was right behind his brother as they neared the pasture and urged their horses forward at top speed. They took the fence in flying leaps. When they came to the boulders the boys had passed on their way to Juniper Field before, they fell into single file and rode along the narrow path through the woods. Arriving at Juniper Field, they circled the airport then slowed their horses to a canter in the town.

Night was falling when they drew rein within sight of the county historical museum. Frank maneuvered close to Joe. "The gang might hear us coming," he warned. "We'd better go the rest of the way on foot."

They dismounted and tied the horses to a tree, then they sneaked through to the edge of the woods. The museum was dark except for a light in one room.

"That's the west wing," Joe noted. "The one Clay said was closed for repairs."

"Well, something's going on in there now," Frank pointed out.

Reaching the museum grounds, they climbed a picket fence and crawled toward the building on their hands and knees. They moved along cautiously in case a member of the gang was standing guard. Judging that the coast was clear, they rose to their feet and flattened themselves against the wall on either side of the lighted window. Gingerly they peered around the frame into the room.

It was filled with weather vanes!

"There's the *Flashing Arrow!*" Joe whispered, "and the *Galloping Rider* is right next to it!"

Crow Morven and Ed Bryle were shifting the weather vanes and stacking them near the door. "We can load these up in a hurry," Bryle declared as he placed the *Flashing Arrow* at the end of one stack.

"We sure fooled the Hardys," Morven gloated with an evil grin. "They never caught on when I cut the phone line from the barn to the house. And they didn't figure out that I sneaked into the house and doped Hammerley's cocoa. Too bad I couldn't get into the kitchen and destroy the evidence. But that dratted Mrs. Smith locked the window after I unlocked it."

"Those nosy kids!" Bryle complained. "I'd feel better if my time bomb had gone off sooner and done away with them. As long as they're around, there's no telling where they'll turn up next!"

Morven nodded. "That's true. But there's nothing we can do about it now."

Having finished shifting the weather vanes over

to the door, the men returned to the center of the room where there was a table flanked by a number of chairs. They sat down. Morven tilted his chair onto its back legs and placed his feet on a corner of the table. "Wanna play a game of poker while we're waiting?" he asked.

"Why not?"

Frank nudged Joe. "We've got enough evidence to blow the whistle on them. Let's get the police before they clear out of here!"

The Hardys were about to move when Frank pulled Joe back against the wall. A beam of light flashed past them. Instinctively, they froze to avoid being seen.

"It's a headlight," Frank whispered. "A truck's coming."

The vehicle eased up to the museum through the darkness and stopped at the door of the west wing. The driver got out. He was the tall man wearing a black beard and dark glasses!

Climbing the stone steps, he knocked on the door; first three slow knocks, then two rapid ones, and finally three slow ones again.

"That must be the gang's signal," Joe thought to himself.

A chair scraped on the floor inside. Footsteps approached the door. When it opened, Morven was standing there.

"Hi, boss," he said.

The newcomer went into the museum. The Hardys returned to their post at the window and watched him sitting down. Unlacing his heavy shoes, he took them off and pushed them under the table, revealing as he did so that they were specially built with soles about three inches thick.

He drew a regular pair from beside the chair, put them on, and stood up. Now he was of medium height. He grabbed hold of his black beard on one side and stripped it off with a single motion. Then he removed his dark glasses and replaced them with steel-rimmed spectacles, which he pushed up on his forehead.

"Joshua Korbo!" Frank and Joe gasped the name as they recognized the auctioneer.

Korbo tossed his beard and dark glasses aside. "I won't need these anymore," he said. "Our weather vane caper in this county is over. I'll use a different disguise the next time. We go into action again a hundred miles from here after the heat's off."

"Good idea," Morven said. "I could use a little vacation in between."

"We'll use the same system," Korbo went on. "Each time, I'll prepare a paper with a hex sign identifying the weather vane and the place to hide it. Then we truck it on to Chesapeake Crossing."

He took a list from his pocket, went over to the weather vanes, and checked them off with a pencil.

Morven and Bryle watched him in silence. They seemed afraid of an explosion if Korbo found any of the stolen items missing.

"All here," he said with satisfaction after a moment or so. "I'll bring in my fence now so we can move our goods."

He went to the door and called out, "Bucky! Come in and have a look!"

A man got out of the truck, walked up the stairs, and entered the room. He was the desk clerk from the Sunset Motel!

Clay didn't have to sneak into the motel with the cassette, Joe now realized. All he had to do was walk in and hand it to Bucky! Some motel clerk— he's an international smuggler!

Bucky looked over the stacked weather vanes. "This is a good haul. The *Flashing Arrow* and the *Galloping Rider* will go for about twenty grand apiece. The rest are nearly as valuable. I'll be able to fence them abroad. My contacts will buy every American weather vane I can send them. And all the classified Pentagon documents from Washington!" Bucky added with a grin.

"No more documents from now on," Korbo said.

"What are you talking about?"

"Wickerson got caught and arrested last night. Not only that, the Hardys were at Barren Island and freed Clifford Hunter!"

172

"What!" Morven and Bryle were flabbergasted.

"If you hadn't failed with your bomb plot," Korbo said to Bryle, "we'd be in better shape. Wickerson is a real threat to us now if he talks, and so is Hunter, not to mention those nosy detectives!"

Bucky became nervous. "Let's load up as fast as we can. I have a cabin on the beach at Chesapeake Crossing where we can store the goods safely until we see the midnight signal out on the bay. Then I'll deliver them by powerboat."

Korbo turned to Morven and Bryle. "Okay, start moving the stuff out to the truck."

Frank and Joe put their heads together underneath the window. "You go for the police," Frank said in a low tone to his brother. "I'll watch the crooks."

"Oh no!" boomed a voice behind them. "You're both going, ahem, inside!"

20

The Flashing Arrow *Clue*

Whirling around, the Hardys were confronted by Gaspard Clay and two other men brandishing ax handles at them.

"Up the steps!" Clay commanded. "And no tricks or we'll use these on you!"

Frank and Joe, seeing they had no alternative, entered the west wing of the museum, closely followed by their captors.

"The Hardys!" Korbo exploded. "Where'd you find them?"

Clay explained how he had caught the boys listening outside the window.

"Then they must have heard everything we said!" Korbo grated.

"Doesn't matter, boss," Morven rasped. "Now we can get rid of them for good."

Bryle scowled at the boys. "The time bomb I planted on your powerboat should'a done you guys in a couple of days ago!"

"You made the mechanism too loud," Frank told him. "We heard it when we cut the engine."

"Well, you only postponed your fate," Clay smirked. "I tried to warn you off the weather vane case and told you the hex was on you, but you wouldn't take the hint. Now you'll pay for it!" He turned to Morven. "Tie 'em up. We'll drop them into the Chesapeake Bay!"

Morven produced a rope and shoved the boys against the far wall next to the door to the main building. He tied their ankles and bound their hands behind their backs.

"Can't we at least sit down?" Joe spoke up. "It's not our intention to make you comfortable," Korbo replied sarcastically. "Not only are you going to stand up, you're going to shut up!" He turned to Morven. "Gag 'em, Crow!"

Morven tied handkerchiefs across the boys' mouths. Then he drew a four-pronged grappling iron from under a table. "This is what we used the night we snatched the *Flashing Arrow*," he said with an evil grin. "It'll sink you in the bay when we get there!" He looped the rope with which he had tied their ankles around the prongs of the grappling hook so it served as an anchor holding them in place.

"Now we'd better start loading the truck," he suggested. "We don't want to waste any more—"

A police siren in the distance interrupted Morven's sentence.

"The cops!" Korbo exploded as the sound grew louder. "They're coming this way. Everybody duck!" He ran to the door and locked it, then snapped off the light, plunging the room into darkness. Seconds later several squad cars roared up and surrounded the museum.

"You cannot escape!" Mr. Hardy announced through a bullhorn. "Throw down your weapons and come out with your hands up!"

There was a moment of stunned silence, then Korbo recovered his wits. "We have Frank and Joe Hardy in here, and we'll blow their heads off unless you let us go to our truck and get out of here!"

"You want a murder rap against you in addition to all the other charges?" Mr. Hardy demanded.

"I want to get out of here and I have enough bullets for all of you!" Korbo screamed in rage.

"What if your bluff doesn't work?" Morven hissed. "Maybe we should try to escape through the east wing!"

"Shut up!" Korbo grated. "Don't you realize they've surrounded the whole place?"

Frank tugged on his bonds in frustration. If only he could tell his father that the gang was unarmed! As he moved, he felt something scraping his back. "Feels like a light switch," he thought. He remembered a signal he had once worked out with his father when they were staking out a hut in the woods. "The coast is clear" was transmitted by turning his flashlight on, off, and on again in equal intervals. His heart pounded as he manipulated the switch behind him. Would it work?

Suddenly the room was bathed in light. Before the gang could figure out what had happened, Frank turned the light off, then on again. Mr. Hardy instantly recognized the message, and moments later the police broke through the door. "Hands over your heads!" they commanded. Stunned and dazed, the criminals obeyed.

Mr. Hardy and John Hammerley had followed the officers, and the Bayport sleuth untied his sons.

"After dropping Clifford Hunter off in Washington, I flew out to Lancaster and called Mr. Hammerley," their father explained while he took off their gags. "He told me you had ridden into town and he asked me to meet him at police headquarters. Then we decided to check on the museum."

"Good thing you did," Frank said with a sigh of relief. "We were to be dropped into the bay after the crooks got away."

The police chief was amazed when he recognized the members of the gang. "Joshua Korbo and Gaspard Clay were two of the most respected men in the county!" he exclaimed.

"That's how they got away with it," Joe pointed out. "Nobody suspected them, including us."

An idea struck Frank. "Clay," he addressed the curator, "I bet you followed us that day we found you crabbing."

Clay looked sullen. "Why should I tell you anything?"

"Because if you cooperate, things will go easier for you," Mr. Hardy said. "However, I want you to understand that you don't have to answer without consulting with your attorney first."

Clay realized he was defeated. With a helpless shrug, he looked at Frank. "Yes, I followed you. I saw your powerboat explode and realized you swam ashore. So I stopped to crab, ahem, where I thought you'd hear me and come down for a look. If you had ridden back with me to the marina, I might have disposed of you on the way. Unfortunately, you refused."

"Not so unfortunate for Clifford Hunter," Frank said pointedly.

Clay glared at the boys. "You knew about Chesapeake Crossing from the paper Bryle dropped in the helicopter. But how did you know enough to come to the museum tonight?"

"Easy," Joe replied. "You told us."

"What do you mean?"

Joe described how Frank had discovered that the squeaky voice on the cassette was Clay's. "So," he added, "we thought something must be up at the museum."

Korbo seethed. "You guys know everything, don't you!"

"We know that you had a perfect cover," Frank replied. "As an auctioneer, you could travel around the county and list the weather vanes. Then you sent your hoods to steal the best ones."

"Also," Joe added, "your auction gave you a good place to hide the antiques. They looked like items you intended to sell. By the way, how did you get involved with Bucky?"

"We were in the rackets together," Korbo admitted. "Then he set up a fence in Chesapeake Crossing. One day he told me he could handle the coming thing in stolen goods—valuable weather vanes. So I went into heisting weather vanes for him."

"And since Clay was a member of your gang," Joe spoke up, "you could use the museum as a warehouse."

"Right. And everything was terrific," Korbo snarled, "until you came snooping around. I had to switch to the helicopter because you were in the barn loft and Morven couldn't get at the *Flashing*

Arrow that night. I piloted the chopper and Bryle snatched the weather vane with his grappling hook right from under your noses!"

Bryle guffawed. "I can still see you two climbing over the roof. But we got there first. We didn't even need Crow's signal."

The light dawned on Frank. "So that's what you were doing," he accused Morven, "when we jumped you in the barn."

Morven scowled. "I thought you would be asleep. I was supposed to give the exact location of the place with a flashlight. When you caught me, I told you I was looking for my jacket."

"Anyhow, we got away with the *Flashing Arrow*," Korbo continued, "and landed at Juniper Field. My plan was for Bryle to drive it to Chesapeake Crossing, but he couldn't find the paper with the hex sign. I realized he must have lost it in the chopper while operating the winch. So I told him to take the weather vane to the museum instead."

"Then you went back to the auction where we saw you the next day, packing up," Joe continued.

Korbo nodded. "I put on my disguise when you left and drove to Chesapeake Crossing to confer with Bucky."

"We know," Frank said. "We saw you in that big black car and chased you."

Joe changed the subject. "Why did Wickerson get into the spy business?"

"He needed money," Korbo replied. "He lost a lot at the racetrack, so he sold his valuables. He had a good collection of antiques, and I auctioned them off for him. Eventually they were all gone, but he was still hard up.

"One day he told me he had access to classified Pentagon documents relating to navy research and asked me if I could sell them. Naturally I checked with Bucky. He has a lot of foreign contacts. Bucky said yes, and Wickerson forced Hunter into taking the MASUB plan from the Pentagon files."

"Where is the document now?" Frank asked.

Bucky, who was frightened to the point of panic when Korbo revealed his past, pointed a finger at the auctioneer. "He has it!"

"Hand it over, Korbo!" Mr. Hardy ordered.

"I don't have it. You can search me if you like."

The police went through his pockets, but they were empty, and a search of the other gang members failed to produce the Pentagon plan.

"Maybe he hid it somewhere in the museum," Frank suggested.

The officers searched the building thoroughly without finding the blueprint, however, and further questioning of Korbo netted no answer. Suddenly Joe had an idea.

"Wait a minute!" He lifted the *Flashing Arrow* and placed it on the table. Then he unscrewed the arrowhead and pulled it off. He inserted his finger into the hollow tube and maneuvered it upward until the end of a paper began to show. Smiling, he withdrew it with his thumb and forefinger. He unrolled it and held it up. It was the MASUB blueprint!

"How did you know?" Frank asked his brother.

"I remember unscrewing the hollow arrowhead when we were on the barn roof, and it hit me that a document could be rolled up and hidden in there!"

"Excellent deduction!" Mr. Hardy praised his son. "You've done the U.S. Navy a great service!"

The police took the gang to headquarters, and Mr. Hardy and John Hammerley accompanied them. Frank and Joe, meanwhile, went back to their horses.

"Do you think we'll ever get another good case to work on?" Frank asked his brother on the way.

"I sure hope so!" Joe replied. "Life would be dull without mysteries."

Frank nodded. He had no idea that soon they'd be called upon to solve *The Apeman's Secret*.

When they climbed onto their horses, Joe suddenly grinned. "One thing I could do without, though."

"What's that?"

"The hex!"

Don't miss these new mystery stories

THE HARDY BOYS™ 59
Night of the Werewolf
by Franklin W. Dixon

THE HARDY BOYS™ 60
Mystery of the Samurai
   Sword
by Franklin W. Dixon

THE HARDY BOYS™ 62
The Apeman's Secret
by Franklin W. Dixon

NANCY DREW® 57
The Triple Hoax
by Carolyn Keene

NANCY DREW® 58
The Flying Saucer
   Mystery
by Carolyn Keene

Plus exciting survival stories in

The Hardy Boys™ Handbook
Seven Stories Of Survival
by Franklin W. Dixon
with Sheila Link

*Available in Wanderer Paperback and
Wanderer Reinforced Editions*